A Tom Jackson Legal Thriller

ROD BESLEY

Know Your Enemy

First published in Australia in conjunction with IngramSpark and Lightning Source.

Please be aware that this novel has been written in **Australian English** and uses Australian language, spelling, grammar and punctuation conventions. These are notably different to American, Canadian and even British language conventions.

Cover designed by Judith San Nicolas
Printed and bound in Australia by IngramSpark
Prepared for publication and edited by The Erudite Pen (theeruditepen.com)

A catalogue record for this book is available from the National Library of Australia

NATIONAL LIBRARY OF AUSTRALIA

Know Your Enemy: A Tom Jackson Legal Thriller (Book 1)
ISBN 9780645902709
E-ISBN 9780645902716

Dedication

I dedicate this book to you, Karen, my one true love and soulmate.
Your enduring love and endless patience are my greatest strengths.
Your husband, Rod.

Prologue

Monday, February 15, 2016

He found himself sitting in the boardroom and staring into many angry faces. Tom Jackson felt uneasy, not something he was accustomed to as the firm's most successful transaction lawyer. He wondered how he'd come to be in this situation, and had an overwhelming sense that he'd been completely and uncharacteristically blindsided.

Then the attack began. His accuser Miles Fletcher, fellow law partner at Ridgeway Mason, launched into an eloquent and obviously pre-prepared series of claims about Jackson's recently observed behaviour. The implication was clear: Jackson had inappropriately accessed and misused confidential documents to the detriment of all present, as well as their fellow law firm partners. The accuser's co-conspirator Roger Everingham chimed in on cue, reinforcing all that had been said and claiming Tom had met with a consultant to a key competitor armed with the confidential documents. The only reasonable conclusion that the four other partners could draw was that Jackson was involved in a plan to defect to the competitor, taking clients, valuable firm know-how and resources with him.

Tom Jackson looked to the others present for support, self-assured in the knowledge that he was a longstanding and well-respected member of the firm, only to find none. His colleagues seemed to be completely in sync with all that had transpired so far in the meeting. It was almost as if they had rehearsed and, to the extent they could, scripted the events that were unfolding.

He wondered again how he could have allowed himself to be led into this predicament. For a brief moment, Tom reflected on his recent separation from his wife. He had been devastated and was now painfully aware that her departure had affected him more than he'd been prepared to admit.

His meeting with the consultant was a rare mistake. He knew that now. As flattering as it was, he had not thought it through, nor had he taken appropriate precautions to choose a suitable location for that meeting. How his trouble-making accuser and co-conspirator came to know about the meeting was no longer relevant. They knew, that was all that mattered.

Jackson was brought back to the present as each of the others spoke in turn, repeating the accusations and expressing their outrage.

Usually well prepared for any meeting, Tom referred to the comprehensive file notes he'd brought with him in anticipation of what he thought the meeting was to be about. In another rare mistake, he had completely misjudged this. How had his wife's departure affected him so much? He used to eat fools like Fletcher and Everingham for breakfast. Now they had the jump on him.

As Jackson fumbled through and read passages from his notes on recent adversarial meetings with the two primary attackers, Fletcher spoke over him, launching into phase two of the attack. The documentary evidence his accuser presented to the meeting was intended as further proof of the alleged, and, if proven, highly self-destructive behaviour. Jackson knew nothing about any such documents. There weren't any, and the 'so-called' facts that were being presented at the meeting were a complete fabrication. Tom was furious.

The meeting took a turn for the worse as other partners joined the verbal attack. It was as if they all now could sense the bloodletting that had commenced, and, like a pack of wild dogs with the scent of fear and blood in their nostrils, they collectively bayed for more.

Jackson could now see that this had all been carefully orchestrated by his primary attackers. They had always been jealous of his success

2

within the firm, and had made numerous attempts in the past to diminish his professional and personal standing. This meeting was an attempt to escalate events with the support of the others present, to further enhance their own prospects within the firm.

A more senior partner among the others suddenly came to his senses and called a halt to the proceedings, suggesting, somewhat optimistically, that all that had taken place in this meeting should remain between those present. The suggestion was not to stop the bloodletting and protect Tom, but to rein in the meeting as it had gotten out of hand and was becoming unprofessional.

Not likely, Jackson thought as he gathered his paperwork and left the room. He had the presence of mind to also grab the so-called incriminating documents that had been thrown at him. Tom wanted to discuss these with a colleague who'd offered to attend the meeting in support. *Another error*, he thought with the benefit of hindsight, *to decline such a sensible offer.* But he hadn't expected to be blindsided by fabricated documentation. Fletcher and Everingham were certainly out for his blood.

Equipped with all the information, including the contrived documents, he stormed into his colleague Max Grenfell's office. Max was able to quickly establish, with the aid of the firm's IT experts, that the suggestion Tom had created the documents at all, or with any malintent, was a fabrication. The IT experts confirmed that nothing they'd found suggested the documents had been created by or for him.

While it appeared that digital tracks had been well covered, further investigation would be required to discover the true source. Even though it was 2016, and forensic analysis processes had advanced significantly over recent times, it would be a laborious process to rule out each potential source one by one. Max Grenfell left it at that with IT, content in the knowledge that Jackson had been exonerated and ruled out as a source of the documents. Max concluded that it was all designed to aid in the process of discrediting and demoralising Tom, resulting in his departure from the firm, either by direction or voluntarily.

Senior law partner Max Grenfell was then able to present the facts and circumstances to each of the others who had been present at the meeting, and each in turn immediately distanced themself from what they now admitted amounted to an ill-conceived attempt at a character assassination. Jackson's accuser and co-conspirator had been deprived of what they'd thought was a credible opportunity to oust him from the firm, and once again found themselves ostracised from the mainstream of the partnership.

But Tom Jackson's exoneration was going to be very short lived indeed.

Chapter 1

Twelve months later (February 20, 2017)

DAY 1 (Monday)

Arriving early at Ridgeway Mason as he usually did, Tom Jackson was preparing for a critical meeting of a key client's board of directors. He collected his notes and headed to the bathroom, taking a moment to again reflect on the reasons why Mary, his wife of almost twenty years, had left him twelve months earlier. Washing his hands, he absentmindedly looked at his reflection in the mirror. At forty-three years of age, he had been told by many that he was charismatic and portrayed an air of authority and leadership. In the moment, it was not lost on him that his tall, athletic physique, dark hair showing a hint of grey at the temples, and easy-on-the-eye looks had resulted in many advances over the years from women of all ages. His estranged wife was aware that he had given in to the temptation, and probably on more than one occasion. It was no excuse, he reminded himself, that such occurrences had only happened recently, and that he'd never carried on any extramarital relationship for any length of time. They were mostly short flings, but he could hardly blame her for leaving him, even though there had been other red flags in their marriage that they had both turned a blind eye to until it was too late.

5

Jackson collected his thoughts before addressing the high-powered board of directors of Pacific Property, an extremely successful owner and developer of property throughout the Asia–Pacific, based in Brisbane, Australia. Having been a long-term partner in the Brisbane office of the respected Sydney-based law firm Ridgeway Mason, Tom had been in this position numerous times before. But this time was different. Something was bothering him. Jackson had been a transaction lawyer for over twenty years and had developed a sixth sense for detecting anomalies, particularly when it came to sources of finance. He had on many occasions identified potential fund sources as questionable and most likely linked to criminal activity.

Tom needed to understand more about the financial aspects of this deal, and those involved, before he could determine with any certainty if something was amiss. His role for now was to update the board on recent developments in the key transaction they had retained Jackson and his firm to undertake: The transaction to finance and jointly redevelop almost an entire and very tired city block in the Brisbane CBD into a mixed-use commercial, retail and residential multi-tower development, which would redefine that part of the CBD.

Pacific Property's chair of the board, Roslyn Green, looked uncomfortable. Ros was a highly intelligent former lawyer who had successfully made the switch to corporate boardrooms. She was a couple of years older than Jackson and had also kept herself in good shape with regular visits to the gym. Her straight platinum blonde hair curled under just above her shoulders, and her trademark red-rimmed glasses made her stand out in any crowd.

'Go ahead, Tom. What's the latest?'

Jackson looked around the table once more and began. 'We are progressing well with negotiation of commercial terms and key documents. As each of you is aware, HK Investments has offered to purchase a sixty per cent interest in your key strategic site in Edward Street, Brisbane, for $300 million, and to fund the entire development cost of $450 million for the additional buildings on the site. Pacific's forty per cent share of the projected end value of $1.5 billion will result in a significant uplift of $400 million over the four-year life of the project, an eighty per cent return on capital invested. HK's return over the same period amounts to a twenty per cent return on capital invested. I know that's a lot of detail, and detail you're all very familiar with, but I have a purpose in reiterating it at this meeting.'

'That's good business for us. An eighty per cent uplift,' said Peter Tomlinson, a little too eagerly for Jackson's liking. Peter had only recently joined the board, and Jackson thought he was overconfident and arrogant. He was in his early sixties with a pinched face and limited remaining amounts of wispy grey hair.

'Continue please, Tom,' urged Ros.

'While I acknowledge the commercial elements of the deal should not strictly be my concern, I do have some doubts about the numbers.'

Peter moved to interject, but Ros silenced him with a steely look.

'I understand that HK Investments has been looking for an opportunity of this magnitude for some time now in Australia,' continued Jackson, 'but this looks to be an extremely favourable outcome for Pacific. An eighty per cent uplift on initial value, versus a twenty per cent return on investment for HK.'

'Why would we care about that, so long as it's appropriately documented by you, Tom, as we expect it will be?' said Richard Black, the chief executive officer and managing director of Pacific. Black was a short man who wore circular glasses, tailored suits and handmade shoes.

'I'm inclined to agree,' chimed in Ros, and the four other directors around the table nodded in unison.

Jackson stood his ground. 'My concern is that the deal looks almost too good to be true from Pacific's perspective. Before any of you comment about the unchallenged negotiating skills of Richard and his team, which I acknowledge, it is my obligation to let you know if I thought anything didn't look quite right. There is a great deal of global money laundering these days, and I've seen some highly sophisticated attempts in recent times to utilise similarly large sums, from suspicious sources, in real estate transactions in this country. Real estate investment in Australia offers a superior return to that on offer in most western nations, accompanied by a high level of sovereign certainty. Conversion to property is a convenient means of legitimising funds derived from illegal activities. I think it would be appropriate to undertake further investigations into the financial integrity of HK. Are you happy for me to do so?'

To Jackson's surprise, he received hostile glares from five of the six board members seated around the table. But not from Ros Green. As a former lawyer, she understood the issues and was happy for Tom to investigate further to ensure they weren't heading down a long and difficult journey with the wrong party.

'I think that's a sensible thing to do,' said Ros. 'Can you carry out the checks in parallel with the document negotiation process?'

Jackson assured her and the board that he could.

'Then I think we'll let you get back to your office to progress this as quickly as you are able to, please,' affirmed Ros.

As he collected his paperwork and prepared to leave, Jackson sensed a general uneasiness within the room. What stood out were the icy looks he received from both Peter Tomlinson and Jennifer Armitage who, at thirty-five, was the youngest and also a relatively new member of the board. As he walked out the door, he could hear discussions recommence among the directors, and he thought the tone had shifted significantly from that which had prevailed when he'd first walked into the room.

Chapter 2

As Jackson headed back to his office, three blocks away in Brisbane's central Mary Street, he found his unease about the deal growing. He wondered why most of Pacific's board, in particular Peter and Jennifer, had seemed so hostile towards his suggestion that he investigate the financial authenticity of HK Investments.

Tom put those thoughts aside temporarily so he could focus on other tensions at his firm. He was heading back to a meeting of the twenty-five partners in the Brisbane office, and he was not expecting it to be an easy meeting. Recent financial budgeting processes had caused significant tensions amongst the 150 or so partners across all three offices of Ridgeway Mason in Brisbane, Sydney and Melbourne. The legal market had altered since Jackson had begun practising. There were now many more students studying law in this country than there were practising lawyers. This at a time when the amount of work available for top-tier law firms was declining, as were the amounts sophisticated clients prepared to pay for that work.

His first port of call on returning to the office was to see his trusted colleague and friend, Max Grenfell. Max was a little older than Tom. He had been at the end of his law degree when Tom had commenced his at the same university. They had reconnected at Ridgeway Mason and had spent the majority of their careers together there. Grenfell was highly intelligent and at times very intense, with an unpredictable sense of humour. His closely shaven head, offset by his reddish moustache, belied the fact that he was as tall as Jackson. Grenfell's penchant for contact sports meant that most of the time he was somewhat comically displaying a cut, graze or bruise on his head or face, and his pale complexion amplified the effect.

He and Max had formed a close working relationship over the years, and their conversations were what Jackson called unguarded. They could talk openly about most things without the need to be cautious about what the other person was thinking, or, more relevantly, plotting against them.

'How did the meeting at Pacific go?' Max enquired.

'Not quite as I anticipated,' Jackson replied, concerned. 'I detected a level of unhappiness, bordering on hostility, amongst board members. I think there's more to this deal than meets the eye, making it all the more important for me to initiate independent investigations into the finances of HK Investments.'

Max nodded his assent, but redirected Jackson's attention to the imminent partners' meeting. 'Have you thought any more about how you plan to deal with the hostile collective at this evening's meeting?'

Max was referring to a group of six partners who seemed to have developed a common interest in seeking to cause Jackson's demise as a partner of Ridgeway Mason. Jackson had considered this development over and over again. He found himself wondering why those in a legal partnership could not see the logic in working together to share contacts, ideas and skill-sets to grow the business for the collective benefit of the partnership and those who work for the business. The undeniable conclusion was that many of the partners, and in particular those in the so-called hostile collective Max had referred to, were professionally envious of and felt threatened by Jackson.

While Tom enjoyed universal respect amongst the partners, including those in the other two interstate offices, many were fearful of the tough professional standards he set and the financial outcomes he consistently achieved. These partners thought they would be better off (and some may even prosper) without Jackson. Tom thought that this was a naïve and blinkered view of reality, and that it said more about the insecurity of many in the profession than anything else – an opinion Max shared in common with him.

Jackson was usually an extremely good judge of character, but in what seemed to be a hastily convened meeting of the hostile six just twelve months prior, had been completely blindsided by a carefully scripted but completely unwarranted attack on him both personally and professionally. And at a time when Jackson was trying to adjust to the fact that his wife had just left him. Talk about kicking someone while they were down.

Never again, Jackson thought silently to himself, and then out loud to Max he said, 'Let's go and do battle again with our fellow business proprietors.'

Max grinned and joined Jackson as they headed off to the meeting.

Chapter 3

Having survived another covertly hostile partners' meeting, Jackson headed home to an empty house. On the way home he reflected on how he and Mary had met in their teens and married in their early twenties. He understood why she had left him, but hadn't yet given up hope of getting back together.

Mary Jackson was an accomplished forensic accountant and Tom had an unwavering respect for her and her counsel. He had sought her counsel sparingly during the last twelve months but decided that he needed to do so again on the Pacific deal. As he dialled her number, he pictured her blue-green eyes and her friendly smile, framed by brown hair with blond streaks, cut short just below her ears.

'Tom. I wasn't expecting to hear from you.'

Jackson winced a little at the slightly bitter tone in her voice. 'I understand, but I was hoping you wouldn't mind if I bounced something work-related off you.'

After a brief pause, she said, 'Okay, what have you got for me.'

Jackson wondered if he was doing the right thing here. He knew it was too early to attempt any kind of reconciliation and quickly explained that he valued her opinion and would appreciate her input on something that was bothering him. He took her lack of response to be an acquiescence and continued with a brief explanation of the Pacific deal, taking care not to disclose any confidential client or transaction specifics. He did mention that there were very large sums of money involved and grossly disproportionate returns projected for the parties.

She mirrored Jackson's thoughts as she spoke. 'As we have often said to each other in the past: If it seems too good to be true, it probably is.'

Jackson thought he detected a note of sarcasm in her voice, and in his mind she was also referring to their relationship. He knew it had been a mistake to call her.

Mary continued. 'I think you may need to be careful with this one, Tom. There's a lot of money at stake and, if your instincts are correct, some serious criminal elements may be involved.'

They exchanged quick pleasantries about health and wellbeing and said goodbye to each other. Jackson thought he detected a measure of care and sympathy for him, but quickly reminded himself that he was not entitled to either and it was most likely wishful thinking on his part.

As he ended the call, his level of apprehension about the property deal grew.

Tom headed to his well-equipped home gym for a workout before dinner. He had studied the martial art Krav Maga at university, and had been disciplined in keeping up his training and fitness levels since then. Krav Maga was the official martial art self defence system of the Israeli Defence Forces, using defence moves aimed at threat neutralisation. How little did Jackson know just how much he was going to need it.

Chapter 4

Jennifer Armitage left the Pacific board meeting and headed for her office in the serviced workplace accommodation conveniently located in the same building as Pacific. Jennifer was well-groomed with dyed jet-black hair, although her complexion suggested her natural hair colour was more something like ash-blonde. She wore thick black eyeliner and mascara, offset by blood-red lipstick, and usually wore a red leather jacket. Jennifer had seen an opportunity and was taking advantage of the current trend towards appointing female directors to correct the large gender imbalance at board level. That's not to say she didn't have the level of competency required for such positions. She was in the process of transitioning from business accountant to full-time professional director, and was very determined to do so successfully.

Jennifer knew she had to make the call, although she was certain it would not be well received. Apprehensively dialling the number, Jennifer reflected again on Tom Jackson's seemingly innocuous comments about the need to verify the source of funds that HK Investments was utilising in the Edward Street transaction.

'This is not a scheduled call,' the Chinese–American voice at the other end of the line barked. 'What is so important that it can't wait until our scheduled weekly call in two days?'

'It may be nothing,' Jennifer responded tentatively, 'but I thought you should know that the transaction lawyer will shortly launch an investigation into – what he termed – the financial integrity of HK Investments.'

There was a prolonged silence on the other end.

'Are you still there?' demanded Jennifer.

'Thank you for letting me know.'

The voice was quietly confident, which unsettled Jennifer.

'We'll handle it.' He hung up without a further word.

Even though Jennifer reminded herself that she had no real cause for concern at this stage, she reflected once again on the wisdom of the arrangement she had agreed to with the previously unknown Chinese man who had a distinctly American accent, three months earlier. Jennifer had only joined the Pacific Property Board three months prior to that, having received an unsolicited invitation to do so from the chair, Ros Green. She had known Ros for some time, and was now getting to know Pacific's CEO Richard Black. Other than for a brief meeting during the initial interview process, she had known very little about Richard prior to the first call from the Chinese businessman. But she was well aware of Black's respected reputation in the property development industry.

When he'd first approached her, the caller had said that he was aware of her growing reputation as an independent director, particularly within the global property investment industry. He had identified himself as James Yeo, and had indicated that he was specifically considering her for other directorship opportunities within that industry. James said he controlled an Asia–Pacific investment fund for a global property investor of around 20 billion US dollars, and that, as he had an indirect interest in arranging finance for the Edward Street project, Richard Black had sanctioned their direct contact. All Yeo had said he needed from Jennifer was a weekly report on the general status of the negotiations of the project between Pacific Property and HK Investments. Up until now, she had discreetly provided the weekly reports without incident and without the need to divulge any information of a confidential nature.

She thought it odd that Yeo had made contact with her and that Richard had not seen fit to mention anything. Perhaps her lack of expe-

15

rience combined with a strong desire to both please Pacific's CEO and to secure more prestigious directorships had clouded her judgement. She had not wanted to confront Richard Black about it, but knew now this was an error and she should have confirmed Richard's authority as part of her basic due-diligence processes. *What a rookie error*, she thought to herself, frowning. *I'm better than that!*

Chapter 5

James Yeo disconnected the call with Jennifer Armitage, mused for a moment, then quickly dialled a number he knew well.

'An issue may have arisen with the Pacific Property–HK Investments deal.'

There was no response, but Yeo expected none. 'I've just had a call from our contact at Pacific. It seems Pacific's transaction lawyer is about to initiate a detailed investigation into HK's finance sources. That's a relatively routine procedure, but this lawyer, Tom Jackson, has an unmatched reputation for identifying – and in most cases eliminating – potential risks in cross-border finance transactions. He's good.'

'What do you suggest?' said the voice on the other end.

While James Yeo had never met the man he was speaking to, they had dealt with each other for many years, and he knew the voice well. Was he imagining it, or did it sound like what he'd just said was through clenched teeth?

'I thought we should just observe for now, and see how this develops,' offered Yeo.

'Not this time,' said the voice, with more volume and determination than James had expected. 'There is too much at stake. We've been working up to this for a long time. I want you to head this off quickly. If Jackson is as good as you say he is, he may uncover something we don't want him to. For now, observe, but observe closely. Let him know someone is watching him. Find out how he plans to go about the investigation, and who he intends to use. Maybe he'll take a different approach if he feels mounting pressure.'

Yeo decided to make two calls after disconnecting. The first he made was to Roger Everingham, one of Jackson's partners in the Brisbane office of Ridgeway Mason. He had dealt with Roger recently, through his contacts in Asia, and knew him to be unscrupulous and open to requests for unusual assistance – for a fee. He also knew there was no love lost between Roger and Tom Jackson.

'I have an interesting matter in which I may need your assistance,' Yeo told Roger on the phone.

'I'm listening.' Roger Everingham was happy to get involved in anything a client or potential client required, so long as it wasn't too difficult and didn't involve too much in the way of complex legal work. He was personable but not very proficient at his chosen profession. Roger had bluffed his way into partnership at Ridgeway Mason using falsified client track record information and references. To date, no one except Jackson had taken him to task on this, and Roger did not take too kindly to what he regarded as unwarranted personal attacks, and in particular from someone with whom he openly competed for the same type of legal work at the firm.

'I would like to engage you behind the scenes to keep an eye on a role Tom Jackson is playing in respect to the Pacific Property–HK Investments transaction,' said Yeo.

'I know the deal. We discussed it briefly at our partners' meeting last month,' responded Roger.

'Is a cash retainer okay?' Yeo knew it would be.

'Of course.' Roger didn't bother to hide his eagerness. Then he added, 'I'll call you every few days with an update, or immediately if I come across anything pertinent.'

Everingham didn't enquire about the task, or the rationale behind it. It was sufficient for him that a significant new client had instructed him to undertake an off-the-books role, and that he'd been provided with an opportunity to work against Tom Jackson's interests.

The second call James Yeo made was to Murray Jensen, a contact he knew in London. Murray was the principal of a London-based operation that had global reach and a proven track record of achieving the almost impossible, without leaving any discoverable traces.

Yeo had met Jensen on a number of occasions, a generally unhappy man in his early fifties. Although not quite six feet, he had a body builder's physique and wore his medium-length West Indian hair in dreadlocks. James was aware that he had grown up on the streets of London and had learnt the hard way how to take care of himself. Jensen was good at intimidating and killing people, both of which he was known to do without hesitation or remorse. His assassins-for-hire operation had been a natural progression and had proven to be immensely successful.

Yeo explained what the issue was, and how he wished Jensen to proceed. The actions Jensen was ordered to take were to be incremental. He must report to and get authorisation from Yeo prior to progressing to the next stage. The fee and methods of communication were agreed, and the conversation was then promptly terminated by James.

When he put the phone down, Yeo reflected that he didn't much like unleashing people like Murray Jensen, or those who worked for him around the globe, but he had absolute confidence that Jensen would undertake the tasks required of him expeditiously and effectively, without question.

Chapter 6

DAY 2 (Tuesday)

There wasn't much traffic on the roads when Jackson left for work that morning, so the run into the city took no more that fifteen minutes. As he reflected on the day ahead, Tom couldn't help noticing a silver AMG Mercedes a few cars behind him. For some reason the car was familiar. Feeling uneasy, he looked again in the rearview mirror, just before heading down to the basement car park of Ridgeway Mason, but the car was nowhere to be seen. *It's nothing,* he reassured himself. *You're just being paranoid.*

*

Max Grenfell arrived in the office not long after Jackson. Their offices were not far apart, and Max usually popped into Jackson's office for a quick chat on the way to his.

'Morning, Tom. How are you planning on going about the Pacific Property investigation?' Max got straight to the point. He'd sensed from Jackson's mood yesterday that this was troubling his colleague.

'Thanks for stopping by,' Tom was quick to respond. 'I was keen to discuss this further with you before proceeding.' He lowered his voice. 'I thought of engaging Jason Jones from JJ Investigations in Sydney.'

'Excellent choice. He's expensive, but aggressively effective.'

Jackson nodded in agreement.

'I presume you'll let Jason know of your reservations about the Pacific–HK deal, on a confidential basis of course, as that may alter the methods of enquiry?'

'Precisely what I had in mind, and what I wanted to discuss with you,' said Jackson. 'I'm relieved you agree this is an appropriate strategy.'

Max gave a thumbs up and headed to his office.

Jason Jones and Tom Jackson had known each for more than twenty years, and were a similar age. Jones had been a few years ahead of Tom in his Krav Maga training when he'd started learning the discipline at university. Jones had been at the same university for two years studying business and finance, but had decided that it was not for him. He had left university to pursue a more active career in the army, and had very quickly worked his way into the special forces. Although he'd left the army some years earlier, he still sported an army-style buzz haircut, which suited his six-foot barrel-chested muscular physique.

Sydney was an hour ahead. Queensland for some reason still stubbornly refused to see the good sense in daylight saving, Jackson mused, dialling Jones' number. The phone was answered on the second ring.

'Jones,' said the familiar voice of Jason Jones, answering his direct line, which not all clients were given.

'Jason, it's Tom Jackson from Ridgeway Mason in Brisbane.'

'Long time no speak. What gives?' replied Jason, straight to the point as usual.

Many people underestimated Jones. While he didn't mince words, he was a brilliant investigator, particularly when it came to unravelling global financial webs. Jones was well-connected globally and had enjoyed a distinguished military career, including three tours of Afghanistan. After leaving the army ten years prior, he'd started his own private investigation business based in Sydney, with an emphasis on finance and fraud. With Jones' military and martial arts background, he didn't take long to implement his plans to expand the business to include personal protection.

21

'I have an urgent job for you. One that I think you'll find interesting.'

'You have my undivided attention, mate,' responded Jason.

After Jackson's comprehensive description of the Pacific–HK Investments transaction, including what he thought were the disproportionate returns, the reactions of some of the members of board, and his heightened instincts about the deal, Jones enthusiastically boomed into the phone, 'Got it. I've taken a note of the entity names and people you mentioned, and will start investigations straight away. I should be able to get a prelim verbal report to you by midday tomorrow. Call or email me if you think of anything, or anyone, else, but let's try and keep written traffic to a minimum for now. Thanks for the call, Tom.' Jones signed off.

As Jackson cradled the office phone, he felt his tension ease a little as he tilted his head back and looked up at the ceiling. At least now he had one of the best in the game looking into this for him, and with the consent of Pacific's board. If anything was amiss, Jones would get to the bottom of it. He'd been doing this for more than a decade, and his network of global contacts was extensive.

Chapter 7

Roger Everingham wasn't much good at being a lawyer, but he had a real skill when it came to quickly unearthing information within the firm that he shouldn't freely have access to. Particularly when he was being paid in cash to do so. By lunchtime, he knew that Jackson had contacted Jason Jones at JJ Investigations in Sydney, and had correctly guessed that this was in connection with the Pacific Property deal. Roger had simply bullied the accountant in the Brisbane office of Ridgeway Mason into providing him with a list of all new payees entered onto the system that morning, backing up the request with a fabrication about wanting to understand which key external consultants the firm was currently engaging.

Early after lunch, Roger telephoned James Yeo. 'Jackson has contacted Jason Jones from JJ Investigations in Sydney. He's about the best there is in terms of unravelling underlying funding sources.'

'I'm aware of his work. Thanks for getting this to me so quickly.' Yeo terminated the call.

Roger thought that a little abrupt, but nonetheless was feeling pleased with himself. He was not sure what this was all about, but all he needed to know was that he might in some way be helping to bring Jackson undone.

He tucked his business shirt into his trousers, in what amounted to a constant but ineffective ritual to detract from his overweight and slovenly appearance. As he walked around to Miles Fletcher's office, which was on the same level, he stroked the pencil-thin goatee at the centre of his chin and ran his hands through his greasy mid-length brown hair to smooth down the remnants of his premature baldness.

Fletcher had been a partner at Ridgeway Mason for around ten years. He wasn't particularly well liked, but, despite his unjustifiably high staff turnover, was tolerated because he had a good corporate client base and was one of the highest billers in the Brisbane office. No one disputed that Fletcher was intelligent, and he was regarded by some as a brilliant corporate lawyer. Even though he was a bit rotund around the middle, he had a more athletic physique than Everingham, and was always well dressed. Both were in their early fifties.

Roger Everingham was well aware of his own shortcomings, but he was clever at identifying people like Miles. People he could enlist to his causes to offset some of his own inadequacies.

It was Miles Fletcher who had been the attack dog at the attempted character assassination of Jackson twelve months earlier. For his part, Miles had finally earned the respect he thought he richly deserved, albeit for a very brief time, and from a group within the firm that Jackson and Max Grenfell had come to view as both ethically and professionally bankrupt.

'I need your help with something involving Jackson,' began Roger as he walked into Miles' office without knocking, jutting out his chin and focusing his beady little eyes on Fletcher.

'Gladly.' Fletcher's countenance brightened, keen to display his eagerness to assist.

'I have a client interested in the Pacific Property deal with HK Investments. They are thinking of doing a similar development nearby,' lied Roger, 'and have asked me to find out what I can about the deal Jackson mentioned at our last partners' meeting that he's working on. I need your help on how to best find out what we can about Jackson's current activities.'

They talked for the next hour and a half, and as he finally left Miles Fletcher's office, Roger congratulated himself on how well he had just manipulated Miles. Again. What they had come up with together would allow Everingham to find out all he needed to know about Jackson's activities with respect to the deal. Among other methods they discussed,

Fletcher knew how to access all time entries on any file in real time. With the comprehensive descriptions that he knew Jackson and his team usually pumped into the system throughout the day, he'd told Roger he could provide him with regular updates.

What Everingham and Fletcher did not expect was that Jackson also had a good working knowledge of the system, including the levels of transparency that management forced them to comply with. This, as well as his inherent distrust of most, meant Jackson was very careful in sensitive matters with both the information he shared with his team and how he and they noted their time-recorded activities on his files.

Chapter 8

It was late on Tuesday afternoon when Jackson's mobile rang. Jason Jones's name flashed on the screen. 'I didn't expect to hear from you until tomorrow,' Jackson said as soon as he answered.

'What have you gotten involved with, you crazy bastard?' Jones sounded breathless, like he'd been running.

'What are you talking about?' Tom sat up straighter in his chair.

'Some bloody strange things started to happen not long after I got on the blower to begin my enquiries into where HK may be getting its dosh from. I had my team start their electronic enquiries at the same time. Some of my contacts are either not available, or too afraid, to speak with me. That's never bloody happened before, mate. On top of that, one of my key techies hit an electronic brick wall. His laptop is fried! I'll press on, Jacko, but I wanted to let you know what's goin' on. I think we should both be careful with this one.'

Jackson stared at his phone for some time after the call from Jason had ended. This didn't sound right. He headed for Max Grenfell's office. But he'd already left for the day, like most other colleagues. He decided not to call him.

Tom returned to his office and locked away some of his files. A daily ritual. Jackson had the very strong view that there were those within the firm who snooped around partners' offices when it suited them. He was certain they were looking for information and opportunities that might assist their own progression within the firm. Tom had long suspected Roger Everingham of engaging in this activity. The bastard. In fact, he had noticed specific evidence of this around the time of his meeting with the hostile collective – as Max called them – last year.

As he headed for his car in the basement, Jackson's instincts were on high alert and his nerves were tingling, although he reassured himself that it was ridiculous to believe that he may be in any danger.

Not long after leaving the firm's carpark, he noticed a silver AMG Mercedes. This time it was parked on the side of Alice Street, but it left the kerb shortly after Jackson passed by. *Surely that's not the same one I saw on the way in that morning,* Jackson thought to himself. It was hard not to be paranoid after what Jones had just told him, and Tom didn't believe in coincidence. He noticed the driver was female, and for some reason that helped him to relax a little, but not much. Their two-car convoy headed down the Alice Street ramp to the freeway.

The AMG tailgated Jackson and roared past at the first opportunity, actually clipping the rear of his car as it did so. Jackson needed all his well-honed driving skills to avoid losing control of his Lexus. The car's intuitive safety system came into play, and he quickly regained control. When he looked ahead, the AMG was gone. *Fuck,* he fumed, *that looked intentional.* He must have hit a nerve with his decision to investigate the deal's funding. He glared in the direction the AMG had taken, his nostrils flaring in anger. *What was that bitch thinking? She could have killed me.*

Chapter 9

Sarina George, the driver of the AMG Mercedes, didn't mean to clip the rear of Jackson's car. A near miss was all she had intended, but she was pleased with herself for hitting him. When Murray Jensen had called her the day before, he'd explained that the client had asked them to apply some pressure to Tom Jackson, albeit incrementally, and to ensure that there would be no doubt in his mind that he was being followed. She wasn't told what this was about, and she didn't need to know. Sarina was good at what she did, and never sought to overcomplicate things by seeking information that was not volunteered.

Sarina had worked for Murray Jensen for almost two years. She had shoulder length dark hair, was of slim build, and was moderately attractive with an unfortunate purple birth mark on her left cheek. In her late twenties, Sarina had been dishonourably discharged after only four years in the British army for violent outbursts. She had a mean streak and was better suited to working for someone like Jensen, whose army contacts kept a close eye out for him for characters of this nature.

Sarina would report to Jensen when she arrived home, via their scheduled daily call. He might be a little cranky at first, but she would assure him that she had not put Jackson in any real danger, and, more importantly, that Jackson would now have the message they intended to deliver.

Jensen was cranky with her, as she had suspected.

'We don't fuck with this client,' he'd ranted. 'They specifically said that we were to incrementally increase the pressure on Jackson, but only after receiving their specific approval to do so.'

Sarina was a little taken aback by his unexpected hostility. 'What's the big deal?' she asked in an almost apologetic tone. She was fearful of Murray, and her fears were well founded. 'It wasn't intentional, but I think he'll get the message. Why don't I hold off a little for now and see what develops?'

'All right, but don't fucking do that again. Stick to the specific instructions I give you, or I'll find someone else who can,' said Jensen, more aggressively this time, and he terminated the call.

Sarina had not heard Jensen snap so quickly before. In the many dealings between them over the last two years, she had not had such a tense conversation with him. She was usually happy to play bit parts in larger schemes. Her role was mostly surveillance for the more senior operatives working for Jensen, who would ruthlessly implement the client's intimidate, maim or kill instructions. The call made her wonder what this contract was all about, and who the key players were.

Chapter 10

Once home, Jackson called the local police station to file an incident report. It took forever for the non-emergency number to answer. In the evenings, the police were usually occupied with what Jackson referred to as the 'creatures of the night'. These were the unusually high proportion of the city's ordinary citizens whose personalities were transformed after dark by drugs and alcohol. A decade ago, this group had been mostly comprised of university students, but these days it increasingly included Mr or Ms Suburbia. Modern-day pressures, largely brought on by continuous technological advances, competitive environments and information overload, caused excessive levels of stress that people sought to relieve at the end of the day by any convenient means available.

'Constable Cotrell, how can I assist?' said the childlike voice at the other end of the phone when it was finally answered.

He sounds no older than fifteen, Jackson thought to himself. 'My name is Tom Jackson. I'm a lawyer and I would like to report a traffic-related incident.'

'No problem, sir. Please describe the incident,' sighed the constable.

Jackson could tell this would likely be a waste of time, but he knew he should at least endeavour to get it on the record.

Jackson described the incident with the AMG Mercedes, including precise details of the time and location.

'No injury to you or damage to the car?' responded Constable Cotrell in a monotone voice.

'No.'

'And while you say you can describe the vehicle, you didn't get a registration number?' the constable went on.

'That's correct.' Jackson knew where this was headed.

'Then there's not a lot I can do about this. I'm sorry, sir. I will make a note of what you've told me, and will file it in the daily log, with your details attached. Hopefully that will be the end of it for you.'

Jackson thanked the constable and terminated the call. He suspected that would not be the end of it. This had to be connected to the investigations he'd commissioned. Cracking his knuckles, he thought about what to do next.

Chapter 11

Roger Everingham had stayed late in the office. He knew Jackson was often last to leave. Everingham had removed his car from the basement car park earlier so it was not obvious to anyone that he was still in the building.

He was congratulating himself on his strategy and his new appointment as he walked into Jackson's office. This was not the first time he'd done this. Hopefully he'd have more success on this occasion than the last in locating something of interest. He was keen to follow up his early report to James Yeo, and wanted access to Jackson's file. Everingham was painfully aware that Jackson kept impeccable file notes of events as they occurred.

He also knew that the senior lawyer had taken comprehensive notes of the meetings he and others had had with Roger prior to him becoming a partner at Ridgeway Mason. It was these notes he'd been looking for in Jackson's office a year ago, without success. If divulged, and believed, the notes would go a long way towards confirming that he'd fabricated and exaggerated evidence of his levels of success in the industry during the interview process. Everingham wasn't sure why Jackson had not brought the notes to light, but he wanted to pursue his agenda to unsettle and discredit him, and hopefully cause him to leave the firm before that occurred. That was the primary reason behind Roger Everingham's motivation to garner support for Tom Jackson's character assassination.

Jackson's office had a sense of order that was foreign to Roger. He stood in the centre of it for a moment, contemplating why anyone would need, or even bother, to be as organised as Tom was. The file he was looking for was not on the desk, nor in the open bookshelves, where he knew Jackson kept his currently active matters. The less active, but still current, matters were in alphabetical order in the cupboards. Not there either.

Everingham noticed two filing cabinets in the corner. *They're new,* he thought to himself as he tried the drawers. They were all locked, much to Roger's frustration. He left hurriedly, hoping that no one within the firm was monitoring the daily security card entry and exit reports to the three building levels that Ridgeway Mason occupied.

He would meet with Miles Fletcher tomorrow to see if he'd come across anything of interest since he'd lucked out.

Chapter 12

George Kim's family had been involved on the fringe of criminal activity for as long as he could remember. They had sent him from Hong Kong to America when he'd reached his teens for an education in finance and business, and in western ways. In his mid-fifties now, he was well entrenched and held leadership positions in most of the family's legitimate and illegitimate activities. Despite his age, he did not yet display any grey amongst his jet-black hair, which he slicked back with hair oil. Short in stature, he knew that he was both feared and respected by those who worked for and with him.

Kim reflected on his call from James Yeo yesterday. He was having lunch at his favourite Cantonese Restaurant, Cornucopia Fine Dining, in East Point on Hong Kong Island.

He and his fellow syndicate members had taken some time to amass the $750 million. They had been searching for an appropriate opportunity to invest those funds, and in doing so, convert and effectively legitimise them. He had also been careful to select Yeo as their conduit. James knew the industry very well and commanded significant respect. He had access to huge sums of investment capital from both corporations and (mega) high net-worth individuals, so his access to the amount in question would not of itself arouse any suspicions.

Many were unaware that James Yeo had a gambling addiction and that his luck had taken a turn for the worse of late. He was indebted to the tune of $5 million to the syndicate, of which George Kim was a senior member. The syndicate operated the largest illegal underground casino in Hong Kong. The syndicate also owned many other businesses including two legal casinos on Macau, but the illegal Hong Kong casino was by far the most profitable.

The fee they had agreed to pay Yeo would clear his debt to them and leave him with a significant surplus. Kim knew that James wasn't aware of the connection between the source of funds and his indebtedness, but of course he was incredibly relieved at being presented with such a timely opportunity to clear his huge gambling debt.

What no one other than Kim knew was that he himself had another direct contact on the board of Pacific Property, not just Jennifer Armitage, Yeo's contact.

He called that contact now. It was mid-afternoon in Brisbane. 'Should we be concerned about this, or is it under control?' enquired Kim as soon as the phone was answered. The recipient knew instantly who the caller was.

'I'm confident the investigations initiated by Jackson will not be detrimental to the cause, but suggest we exercise caution. I think we should take a passive role for now. Let me know if you have a different view,' he said to Kim.

George Kim was angered by this. 'I have a very different view. We've worked hard to put this deal together, so I have taken steps to apply a little pressure to Jackson with a view to encouraging him to not look too deeply into this.'

The voice on the other end was laced with concern. 'I'm not sure that's a good idea. Tom Jackson is not one to be intimidated. In fact, the application of direct pressure may have the opposite effect to the one you intend!'

He didn't ask what steps Kim had taken, not that Kim would have told him.

'We'll see,' said Kim. He ended the call.

Chapter 13

DAY 3 (Wednesday)

Jackson was first in the office again, and having believed he was last to leave last night as all the carparks for Ridgeway Mason had been empty, ran his eye over his office to make sure everything was as it should be. It wasn't. One of the binders in his cupboard was slightly out of place, and he was certain this would not have been the result of any overnight activity by the building cleaners or security. It was happening again. Someone had been in his office looking for something. Jackson was reminding himself that he didn't believe in coincidences when the phone rang. It was Jason Jones.

'Jason. What have you got for me?'

'I've made some real progress overnight, mate,' Jones replied, 'and I've had to exercise extra caution after yesterday's crap. We've confirmed that HK Investments is based in Hong Kong, and have traced its corporate ownership through a web of companies to the Cayman Islands, via London. No luck yet on details of underlying ownership. As you know, we may never get to that info. We'll keep trying, and will let you know how we get on. I've also had a gander at the source of the dosh. HK Investments has not used James Yeo's mob before to raise funds for any project, but this is something that Yeo does for a living. He's been successful for many years at raising significant amounts of money from high net-worth individuals keen to invest in property-related developments in first-world countries. I noticed that this is the first time he's done so for another entity, so I dug a little deeper into Yeo's affairs. This may be a little left field, but rumour has it that he owes a big chunk of dosh to an outfit that owns a few casinos. According to my info, this includes a large illegal one in Hong Kong somewhere, which has supposedly gone undetected for years. Must be still greasing the palms of the local law enforcement, mate. I'm not sure if or how that's connected to what we're talking about, but it could be relevant.'

'I didn't think that still went on.' Jackson was genuinely surprised.

'Huge amounts of money washes around both legal and illegal casinos throughout Asia,' confirmed Jason. 'Has done for decades, and probably will for many more.'

Jackson told Jones about the incident with the AMG Mercedes on the way home the day before.

'Shit. We must have hit a nerve with this one. What do you want me to do from here?'

'Hold off on any further investigations for now,' Jackson replied, 'and don't put anything in writing yet. I need to digest this, and maybe have a chat to the chair of the board on a confidential basis to see how she wants to play it from here.'

'Roger that, mate. Will wait till I hear from ya.' Jason signed off.

Jackson had another good look around his office, checked that his key files on this matter were still locked away where they should be, and that his computer had not been accessed remotely or otherwise overnight. He needed to discuss these latest developments with Max Grenfell.

Max was just arriving as Jackson got to his office. 'I have a scheduled call in five,' said Max, guessing correctly that his friend and colleague was keen to discuss something with him.

'Can you defer it?' Jackson said. 'This is important.'

Max did so, and closed the door to his corner office. 'Shoot.'

Jackson filled him in on the call with Jason Jones the day before, the incident with the Mercedes on the way home and his call from Jones just now. He also told him he thought someone had been looking for something in his office overnight.

'Fuck.' Max rubbed his hands back and forth on his bald scalp. 'Did you report the incident to the police?'

'Sure did,' said Jackson, 'but I'm not expecting anything to come of it. It all happened so quickly that I didn't get the rego number. My immediate concern is what to do with the information I now have.'

'Is there anyone at Pacific Property you trust without question? I know you have a very short list of people in this category, anywhere,' said Max.

'I trust the chair, Ros Green.' Jackson folded his arms. 'I've known her for many years, including when she was a practising lawyer, and have always found her to be honest and reliable. I know most of the board of directors well, but there's a couple of new directors I'm not sure about. Jennifer Armitage and Peter Tomlinson. The CEO, Richard Black, is a bit of an unknown quantity. But I've also known him for a while, and he seems to have an unblemished reputation. He plays his cards pretty close to his chest, however, and I don't think anyone really knows him.'

'Jennifer Armitage is on the board?' Max asked in disbelief, his eyes widening.

'Yes, why the look?' responded Jackson, brows furrowed.

'Watch that one,' said Max. 'She's keen to get on as many boards as she can, and doesn't always play by the rules. I don't know Tomlinson, and I've only heard of Black through his reputation as someone who engages in the ruthless pursuit of profit. For now, I'd keep this information within a very small circle. There is clearly something going on, and from what you tell me there may be someone on the board, and also someone within our firm, working against you. It's probably that bastard Everingham again. I'll keep an eye on him for you.'

'Thanks,' said Jackson. Max was probably right. That slimy prick Everingham was likely involved. Tom reflected again on the wisdom of not informing senior management about his file notes on the meetings with Everingham when he'd first come to the firm. He had thought it best for all concerned to avoid an outright confrontation, content in the belief that karma would dictate Everingham's fate. Tom was pissed off that without Max's assistance he may well have been a casualty of his own inaction. His lip curled as he pictured Everingham's multiple chins and his annoying goatee, giving him a constant look of having dribbled something that he hadn't bothered to wipe away.

He knew he could count on Max's continued support, no matter what happened. During their many years in legal practise together, the two of them had encountered all manner of situations and personalities, and had always had each other's back.

Chapter 14

Jackson returned to his office, closed the door and called Ros Green. Before Ros answered the phone, Tom idly pictured her platinum blonde hair, sensuously slim build, and narrow waist and hips. When Ros had been a partner in a competing law firm, her and Tom's paths had regularly crossed on the opposite side of deals. She was very attractive, and Tom was well aware of the overt sexual chemistry between them.

'Tom, good to hear from you. How are the investigations going?' said Ros. She was always very cheerful and easy going, and as a result, many made the mistake of underestimating her.

'I need to have a chat with you this morning, but not on the phone,' said Jackson. While a little out of the ordinary, Tom was aware that Ros respected his reputation and instincts so readily agreed to a meeting.

'Let's meet at the Rendezvous Café,' suggested Ros. 'It's a little out of the way, but it has good coffee, and at this time of the day will have only the takeaway trade humming. We should be able to have a relatively private chat. Meet you there in fifteen?'

'Done,' replied Jackson.

On the way to meet Ros, Jackson mulled over what he knew so far, trying to decide what to tell her. Everything, he decided. He trusted her professional integrity. More than that, he had enormous admiration and respect for Ros, even though he had been conflicted by his attraction to her while he was married to Mary.

After briefly exchanging pleasantries, Jackson told Ros what had transpired since the board meeting just two days ago. Tom could see that she couldn't believe it.

'How much of this is objectively verifiable?' asked Ros. 'You know we can't present unsubstantiated evidence to the board.'

'I agree. That's why I wanted to have this chat, to see what you wanted to do. Given how quickly things have developed, it looks like someone on the board may be involved. The information my investigator has uncovered, even though some is only verbal so far, is disturbing.'

Ros seemed deep in thought. 'I would like you to have JJ Investigations prepare a report this afternoon, for presentation by you to a meeting of the board that I will convene for tomorrow morning. The report must only contain information that is independently verifiable.'

'That will limit it to the complex web of corporate ownership of HK Investments, which cannot yet be traced to the underlying beneficial ownership. The report will also only be able to describe the uncharacteristic, but justifiable, role that James Yeo has undertaken in arranging the finance,' said Jackson pensively.

'I get that,' responded Ros quickly, 'but we need to keep the board fully informed.'

Jackson agreed, and settled back in his seat with a warm smile on his face, completely at ease in her company.

'What?'

'Oh, nothing really. I was just reflecting on how many years we've known each other. Except for when our paths have crossed at the occasional conference over the years, we've always been too busy to relax and discuss non-work-related things. We should do that sometime.'

Ros did not respond, but Tom could see from the look in her eyes that she would be more than happy to do so.

They checked their electronic calendars to agree on a couple of alternative times for the board meeting tomorrow, and then headed back to their respective offices.

On his way back to Ridgeway Mason, Jackson revisited his conversation with Ros. She didn't seem as concerned as he thought she would be, and he hoped that if something was going on, Ros was not involved.

It would have been completely out of character, but Jackson's experience was that, in the main, people tended to look after their own interests first, no matter what the cost.

Tom called Jones and told him what he needed, and by when. At first Jones protested. He wanted to not just include what he'd heard about James Yeo and what appeared to be happening to Jackson, but also to draw some initial conclusions. When Jackson reaffirmed his concern that someone on the board may be involved, Jason backed off and agreed to present only the verifiable facts in his report.

Chapter 15

Miles Fletcher was keen to uncover something of use for Roger Everingham, his relatively newfound work buddy, so he almost obsessively kept an eye on any time entries Jackson posted on the Pacific Property transaction file. To his delight, Jackson made a note of his conversation with Ros Green, a rare slip up for Jackson, and of the call to JJ Investigations requesting a report for the board. He couldn't wait to tell Everingham, so he rushed around to his colleague's office, humming to himself on the way. The wide grin on his face was out of character. He knew it amplified his large upturned nose and his unfortunate overbite. It's partly why he bleached his hair with peroxide and wore it short with gelled spikes, in the mistaken belief that it would detract from his prominent facial features. Fletcher hovered anxiously by Roger's door while he waited for him to finish a call.

Everingham beckoned to Miles and pointed to a chair. The smug look did not leave Roger's face, nor did he remove his feet from the desk, as he completed the call he was on. Miles was not great at hiding his emotions, and was certain that Roger must know he had discovered something of use in his ongoing vendetta with Jackson.

'You look like the cat who swallowed the fly,' beamed Everingham. 'What is it?'

Miles could hardly contain himself, and did not wish to correct Roger on his cliché error. 'Jackson looks like he had an unscheduled meeting this morning with the chair of Pacific Ros Green, and he's commissioned a report from JJ Investigations for a Pacific board meeting, probably tomorrow.'

'That's fascinating,' said Roger. 'Thanks, mate. Good work. I owe you.'

With that, Miles had the feeling he'd been dismissed, so he meekly rose from his chair and left.

*

Everingham dialled the mobile number he had for James Yeo, a little more apprehensively this time, after yesterday's call.

'What is it, Roger?' Yeo answered on the second ring with a voice instantly signalling to Everingham that he had better not be wasting the man's time. Roger was aware of James' formidable global reputation and was eager to please him but was mindful to avoid pissing him off.

Yeo's response to the information that Everingham had gleaned from Miles was far more civil than the day before. 'Very valuable. Keep up the good work,' James said, in an almost friendly tone, to Roger's pleasant surprise.

He involuntarily wriggled in his chair a little, much like a puppy would when patted by his master. Even though the call had ended, Roger savoured the moment.

Chapter 16

Sarina George had followed Jackson's estranged wife, Mary, to a lunch venue in West End. She had initially been careful to keep her distance while in traffic, in case Tom Jackson had discussed yesterday's traffic incident with her, and she had recognised Sarina's vehicle. It was known that Jackson had kept in contact with his successful wife after their separation, and judging from the circuitous route Mary had taken to West End it was safe to assume the two had discussed this.

Sarina was intrigued and wanted to uncover a little more about what was going on. She had not been tasked to shadow Mary Jackson, and so would not disclose this activity to Murray Jensen. Sarina had rationalised what she was doing by telling herself that if Mary noticed anything unusual, it would serve to escalate the pressure she had been asked to apply to Jackson. Sarina parked her car and followed Mary. In keeping with her trademark overconfidence, she impetuously decided to intentionally bump into Mary to see if she showed any hint of recognition. The widening of Mary's eyes provided all the confirmation Sarina needed, and she quickly left the scene with a playful grin on her face. Sarina was almost certain Mary would call Jackson to report what had just happened, and she did so straight after lunch.

'I wonder what's going on?' Jackson said in a disbelieving voice. 'I'm starting to feel a little concerned.'

'Me too,' responded Mary. 'Do you think we need to be worried about our personal safety?'

They had never experienced anything like this before. While Jackson had on many occasions detected attempts to fraudulently launder large sums of money, each time the negotiations for the potential transaction had been terminated without incident.

'Let's just adopt an "alert but not alarmed" approach to this for now,' said Jackson, deliberating his next course of action.

Chapter 17

On the way home, Jackson collected his pre-ordered takeaway from one of his and Mary's favourite Thai restaurants in Milton. It made him think about his relationship with her, and if he could make things right, or even if he wanted to. He was still thinking about it as he tucked in to the meal when his phone rang. It was Ros Green. While there was nothing between him and Ros, it was obvious to him that there was a connection of sorts between them.

His fleeting feeling of guilt passed as he said, 'Ros, I see the board meeting has been scheduled for 11 a.m. tomorrow. I'll have the report from JJ Investigations to table at the meeting, as you requested. Is everything okay?'

'Are you free to chat, or am I interrupting something?' responded Ros.

'Sure, what's on your mind?'

Ros proceeded to tell Jackson that she had harboured suspicions about the deal between Pacific Property and HK Investments almost from the outset. From the very first board meeting where they'd discussed the deal, it appeared as if one or more of the board members had prior knowledge of aspects of the deal which, at that time, at least as far as she was aware, had not been formally presented to the company.

'When I factor in what you told me earlier today, I am now almost certain that something is going on.'

Ros did not volunteer the identity of anyone she suspected, and Tom knew better than to ask.

'Can we meet later tomorrow, after the board meeting, to work out next steps?'

'Sure,' replied Jackson.

He had lost his appetite a little and leaned back in his chair while he thought about the call with Ros. It made sense to him now why Ros had looked a little uncomfortable at the start of the board meeting two days ago. After some introspection, Tom could again smell the delicious Thai food and he realised how hungry he was. He managed to relax and enjoy the rest of the meal, pondering what tomorrow would bring.

Chapter 18

As soon as Jennifer Armitage saw the meeting request for the 'out-of-sequence' Pacific board meeting to be held tomorrow, her level of concern elevated. She saw from the agenda that a preliminary report from JJ Investigations was to be tabled for discussion. She told herself that, while she did not think she had broken any law, she had engaged in a potential breach of trust by not disclosing her arrangement with James Yeo. Her primary concern was that somehow JJ Investigations had uncovered that relationship, and that this would be included in the report. Rubbing the back of her neck, she blew out a series of short breaths to gain control of her mounting anxiety.

She steadied her breathing and resolved to call the CEO, Richard Black, to see if he knew what was in the report and, if appropriate, to talk through with him the contact she'd had with James Yeo. Jennifer didn't know Richard very well, but knew of his reputation and felt she should be able to trust him. She knew she had to call someone at Pacific and reasoned that Black was the appropriate person. After all, James Yeo had mentioned Richard's name in their first call.

Richard took Jennifer's call straight away. 'Jennifer. What can I do for you?'

'I see we have an out-of-sequence board meeting tomorrow, and that a report from JJ Investigations is to be tabled for discussion.' Jennifer sounded much calmer than she felt. 'Have you seen the report?'

'No.'

'I need to tell you something,' Jennifer continued, now more openly nervous. 'I thought it was nothing at first, but a few months ago I had a call from James Yeo, and he asked me to provide him with weekly reports on the HKI deal. He'd said he had an indirect interest in arranging finance for the deal, and that you had sanctioned his direct contact with me. While I only provided him with information of a basic non-confidential nature, it was naïve of me to do so without your authority. I should have discussed this with you or Ros Green at the time.'

She did not wish to tell Richard about Yeo's suggestion that he had her in mind for other board positions.

Richard interrupted her thoughts. 'Have you discussed this with Ros?' There was a note of alarm in his voice.

'Well, I was going to ask you if I should tell her.'

'No.' Richard's response was quick and firm. 'As I see it, there is no harm done to date. As you know, James Yeo is now heavily involved in arranging finance for the deal, and I'm sure there is nothing more you can tell him that he doesn't already know. I think you should cease any further direct contact with Yeo, and keep this just between ourselves.'

Jennifer was not sure why Richard seemed so calm about what amounted to at least the perception of a breach of trust, but she was very relieved that he was, and agreed to do what he said.

Chapter 19

DAY 4 (Thursday)

Jackson arrived early at work on the Thursday. He noticed to his surprise that two other carparks allocated in the building to Ridgeway Mason were occupied. He recognised the cars owned by his nemesis Roger Everingham, and his sidekick Miles Fletcher. Jackson immediately assumed something was going on. While Fletcher often arrived early, Everingham rarely did. Deciding to steer well clear of his colleagues on the way to his office, Jackson made a mental note to check with Max and see if he had detected anything unusual involving those two.

Tom had checked his emails before he left home, but hadn't yet seen anything from Jason Jones. When he logged on to his laptop, he saw that Jones had sent through the report as promised. He quickly read the report and saw that it contained more information than he had expected it to. Jones had been able to connect the London agent for the Cayman Island entity that appeared to own HK Investments with owners of casino operations in Macau. The report noted that the London agent in question was also the London agent for a Cayman Island entity that owned two casinos in Macau. There was also a suggestion that the two Cayman entities may be related, but that had not been confirmed. While not definitive in isolation, when combined with what Jones had told Jackson the day before, the link to a possible gambling debt by James Yeo became more plausible.

Jackson called Jones to discuss the new information.

'Got lucky, mate,' was Jason's response when queried by Tom. 'I remembered a couple of years ago I was investigating an entity that owned casinos on Macau and traced its ownership to the Cayman Islands, via the same London agent. The two Cayman entities were registered on the same day. Like you, I don't believe in coincidence.'

This really piqued Jackson's interest. *Now we're getting somewhere,* he thought to himself. 'I agree, it would be an extraordinary coincidence,' Jackson said, 'but in isolation it's not definitive.'

'Agreed, but I reckon it's worthy of inclusion in the report, just as a statement of fact, without any accompanying speculation.'

Jackson agreed and said he'd get back to Jason with further instructions once he himself had received directions from Pacific's board.

He made the decision not to email the report to either Ros or any other member of the board. He'd table it at the beginning of the board meeting and carefully observe the reactions of each board member as he took them through the report's contents.

Jackson noticed the light adjacent to Max Grenfell's name on his 'frequent contacts' list on the right-hand side of his laptop screen change from red to green, indicating that Max had just completed a call. He quickly headed for Max's office to catch him before he made another call – he was always on the phone – or headed out.

Max was always pleased to see Jackson. 'I was just thinking of coming to see you, Tom. I have a little information on the scumbags, but nothing significant. I've been wondering how things are progressing for you.'

Max then told Jackson that he too had noticed the early start in the office by Everingham and Fletcher. Unlike Jackson, Max did go in search of the pair when he arrived. He had located them in a closed-door meeting room on the floor below, and had thought that odd given that it was early and there weren't many staff around yet. Even though the door was closed, and the external walls were opaque glass, he'd been able to make out their unmistakable silhouettes – both were of generous proportions – and Everingham's whining tone. He couldn't hear precisely what they were discussing, but was able to make out that they were talking about Tom.

'Have a quick look at this,' responded Jackson, handing over a copy of the JJ Investigations report. 'I'm not going to email it to the chair or the CEO. I want to observe the reactions of each director when they see what's in it.'

'Good plan.' Max scanned the contents of the report. 'Holy crap. When you put it all together, this looks to be the real deal. You can't prove it yet, but there is a fair chance of the involvement of some very serious criminal elements here. I don't think you have enough to go to the authorities yet, and you'd need to be very careful how you went about that. What's your current thinking on this?'

'I plan to take it one step at a time. I'll see how the board meeting goes, and will then separately discuss it with Ros Green. At this stage, Ros is the only one I think I can trust on the board, although I don't have any real concerns about either Shaun Ingram or Kevin Lightfoot.'

Shaun and Kevin were both professional directors in the latter stages of their careers, and Jackson had dealt with each on multiple occasions over the last decade. Their reputations were impeccable.

'Good luck. Keep me posted,' said Max as Jackson headed back to his office.

He had a few other matters to attend to before he completed his preparations for the Pacific board meeting.

Jackson met briefly with two of his team members before dialling the number of the Brisbane lawyers representing HK Investments' interests on the deal. They had a prearranged conference call to discuss key outstanding matters in the document negotiation process. This was good timing as Jackson could then shortly update the board on current progress.

The partner handling the matter was a particularly difficult individual, constantly trying to enhance his own image and reputation by routinely conducting all commercial negotiations as an adversarial process. Jackson regularly outwitted such lawyers who, often obsessed with their own importance, lost sight of the key issues. Today's call was no different.

Tom had learnt many years ago that he was usually able to negotiate a better commercial outcome for clients if he put his ego aside and focused on key issues, without emotion.

Chapter 20

On the way to the board meeting at Pacific Property, Jackson silently rehearsed his role, considering how he would react to the many possible scenarios that could develop. He was very interested to observe the reactions of those around the boardroom table to the information that, while underlying ownership of HK Investments had not yet been established, there may be a link to another entity that owned and operated casinos in Macau.

Ros, a stickler for punctuality like Jackson, commenced the meeting precisely at eleven. All six directors were present. Ros didn't look quite as relaxed as usual, and Peter Tomlinson and Jennifer Armitage looked very distracted. Jennifer seemed to be quite uncomfortable. The CEO, Richard Black, had a rather smug look on his face, and the other two, Shaun Ingram and Kevin Lightfoot, wore neutral but attentive expressions.

'We had a couple of significant wins on our conference call this morning with HKI's lawyers,' Jackson began. 'We have a long way to go, but I'll update Richard and Ros with the details later today. I think we're starting to find common ground on most of the key commercial issues.'

'Thanks, Tom. I look forward to seeing the details. Do you have the investigator's report?' asked Ros.

Jackson nodded and distributed the copies of the report from JJ Investigations around the table. He watched each in turn as they scanned through the content. He thought he saw a flicker of concern on Richard

Black's face, but it quickly disappeared as he regained his composure. Each of the other five directors had expressions ranging from concern to outright shock. Jennifer looked positively distraught.

'Take us through the information please, Tom,' encouraged Ros.

'The investigator has so far been unable to ascertain with any certainty,' Jackson emphasised the last three words for effect, 'the underlying ownership of HK Investments, and he is still working at identifying the various sources of HKI's $750 million contribution to the project. As requested by Ros, the report is limited to verifiable facts for now.'

Jackson didn't want to let them know at this stage that Jason Jones had not had any success tracking down funding sources as yet, nor that he may have reached the end of the line with respect to his investigations into HKI's underlying ownership. 'One measure of concern is the possible link to another entity also registered in the Cayman Islands, which owns and operates casinos in Macau.'

'What the hell are you talking about? This is rubbish,' interjected Peter Tomlinson.

Jackson had been so intent on observing all reactions to what he'd just said that he was taken aback by the ferocity of Peter's verbal attack.

'All I see is some coincidence of date of entity registration in the Cayman Islands, and from that you are suggesting, that HKI may be linked to casino ownership? Either shore up what you're suggesting with tangible evidence, or stop wasting our time and money, and get on with the job we hired you to do. This is a great deal for Pacific, and I for one don't want to see it put at risk by inconclusive investigations such as these.'

'That's enough, Peter,' said Ros, forcefully. 'Tom is doing what we asked of him, and is merely sharing with us the progress report from JJ Investigations. I have some concerns about aspects of this and am of the view that Tom should have the investigator continue with their processes. That way, we'll have an understanding of exactly who we're dealing with and how they're being funded. It won't be a wasted effort. A particular level of detail regarding ownership and funding will also be required by the Federal Government's Foreign Investment Review Board. Does anyone else have a contrary view?'

Jackson had been watching the other directors while Ros was speaking. Fleetingly, Richard displayed the same flicker of concern he'd had previously. Shaun and Kevin were calmly absorbing the information and reactions, as was their usual style.

'Maybe we should consider not going ahead with this,' Jennifer piped up. It was almost as if she had started talking before thinking. Seemingly realising that she had unintentionally articulated what she was thinking, she appeared to reconsider her position, and diluted what she'd said by saying that she agreed with Ros' position. 'At least we should have a clear understanding of who we're dealing with and where the money is coming from.'

All present could tell that she was more nervous about this than she should be, and most did not understand why.

'Jennifer, I don't think you should be at all concerned about what you told me yesterday.' All heads quickly turned in Richard Black's direction.

Jennifer's mouth fell open. She couldn't believe Richard was about to betray her trust and expose her arrangement with James Yeo, and was visibly upset.

'Jennifer has been reporting information on the deal to James Yeo on a regular basis, from a time well before we formally knew James had a mandate from HK Investments to arrange funds. I told Jennifer that I was not concerned about that. While I should have disclosed this to the board, Yeo's contact with Jennifer was with my knowledge and consent.'

It was obvious to Tom from Jennifer's dazed look that she was surprised by what Black had just said.

'That's not how it works, Richard,' Peter Tomlinson almost shouted. 'We all need to be clearly across information-sharing channels. There should be none of this fragmented approach to things. These deals are hard enough as it is without any of us being at cross purposes on key relationship matters.'

Shaun and Kevin were vigorously nodding their agreement, and Kevin was about to chime in when Richard rudely cut him off. 'That's enough debate for now. Ros, I want you to glean a common approach about where to from here at board level, and then you and I can meet separately with Tom to talk through aspects of the deal in more detail. I see no point in debating these issues any further at board level.'

Ros looked blankly at Richard, and without further comment agreed in principle with him that the debate had reached a level of detail that was not necessarily appropriate for board-level discussions.

Shaun and Kevin each spoke briefly, deferring to both Ros and Richard, for now, but each urged the continuation of detailed investigations into the ownership of HKI and the sources of their not inconsiderable funding.

Jackson was still digesting the various comments and reactions at the meeting when he realised it had ended with a resolution. He was to ask Jones to continue his investigations for another twenty-four hours, after which a final report should be prepared and sent to Richard Black and Ros Green for distribution to all board members.

Chapter 21

As they left the boardroom, Richard asked Jackson if he could stay and meet with him and Ros to provide an update on the morning's conference call. Jackson agreed, and the three of them headed to Richard's office.

Tom had been contemplating informing Richard of the suspicious events that had been occurring, as well as Jason Jones' speculation about the gambling debt owed by James Yeo. He didn't know Richard very well, nor what role if any he may be playing in what was increasingly looking like a conspiracy to launder illegal monies. He had to find out. Although Richard had remained seemingly neutral in the meeting, Jackson's instincts told him that the CEO may know exactly what was going on. He resolved to add further credibility to the suggestion that HKI and the Cayman casino-owning entity may be linked. He would mention Jason Jones' information that James Yeo was rumoured to have amassed a huge unpaid gambling debt in Hong Kong.

Jackson updated Ros and Richard on the outcomes from the conference call with HKI's lawyers earlier in the day. Both seemed pleased with the results Jackson and his team continued to achieve. Both Ros and Richard indicated that Jackson's reputation was well deserved, and they were glad he was on their side.

'There's something else,' began Jackson.

Richard inclined his head. 'Yes, what is it?' The CEO always gave the impression that you were keeping him from something else more important. This time his aggressive manner seemed a little more amplified.

Ros raised her eyebrows and ever so slightly shook her head, suggesting that perhaps Jackson should not continue. Tom wanted to test if his instincts with respect to Richard Black were correct. A dangerous game, he knew, but he had always thought it was best to know your enemy.

'Jason Jones has uncovered more information but has not included it in his report because he's not been able to independently verify the detail.' Jackson got straight to the point.

Ros' look was one of concern, and Richard's was anger.

'Jason has some great information sources.'

'Continue, Tom,' said Richard through partially gritted teeth, uncharacteristically displaying his emotion.

Jackson pressed on. 'James Yeo has been incredibly successful at raising funds from institutions and high net-worth individuals for his own organisation, but this is the first time he has done so for another organisation. I agree that may not of itself be an unusual progression for Yeo, and I'm sure that his organisation will benefit significantly if the funding deal is fully subscribed and successfully concluded. What is of concern, however, is other information Jones has uncovered. Namely that Yeo is rumoured to have a gambling problem and may have accumulated a very large debt to a Hong Kong-based casino.' Jackson paused for effect. 'And the casino may well be an illegal one, operating right under the noses of the authorities.'

For the first time since Jackson had known him, Richard was speechless. Not for long, however. As Jackson had observed him do in the board meeting, on more than one occasion, he quickly regathered his composure and spoke.

'I suggest you be very careful about that sort of information, Tom. You need to be extremely cautious about who you pass it on to. In fact, I think it may be an error of judgement for you to have told Ros and me. Unless and until you can verify any such outrageous suggestion, I firmly believe that we should treat it as nothing more than unsubstantiated gossip. It would be unwise for any of us, Jones included, to repeat what you've just said.'

Jackson was certain that he'd hit a nerve with Richard Black. Even Ros was surprised by Richard's seemingly dismissive response and the unnecessarily forceful manner in which it was delivered.

'Anything else?' asked Richard in a far more conciliatory tone.

Both Jackson and Ros shook their heads, and, with that, their meeting ended.

Richard hurried off in a different direction to the one Jackson and Ros took. 'That was either very brave, or very stupid. I can't work out which,' whispered Ros, leaning in close to him.

Jackson's pulse quickened a little with their closeness and her warm breath in his ear. He smiled inwardly and responded in equally quiet tones, suggesting that they meet later in the day to talk things through. They agreed a time and venue, and parted company.

*

Jennifer Armitage had remained in the building, and now intercepted Richard Black as he was heading out. 'Can we talk?' she asked in a hushed but desperate tone.

'Walk with me,' grunted Richard.

Outside on the footpath, heading along Edward Street, Richard asked her what she wanted to discuss.

Jennifer thought that the CEO was behaving as if nothing out of the ordinary had happened in the board meeting. She still couldn't believe what he'd done. 'Why did you betray my confidence?' she demanded.

'Grow up.' Richard's response was immediate and aggressive 'I said what I said in there to protect you. Jackson and his investigator Jones may well have uncovered the arrangement you had with James Yeo. I'm hoping what I said in the meeting will throw them off that trail.'

'Thanks, I think,' responded Jennifer, displaying how upset she was. 'But, casinos? What the hell?'

'I would forget you heard that,' responded Richard clenching his jaw.

'I have to talk to my Ian about this,' blurted Jennifer without thinking, again articulating something she had not intended to.

'What's that? What did you say?'

'Nothing, nothing.' Jennifer was almost in tears now.

*

Richard Black knew it was far from nothing. He knew that the reference to Ian was a reference to Jennifer's partner Ian Fox. Ian was a partner in the Forensic Investigation Division of the Brisbane office of Braxton Bartholomew, a global accounting firm. What had James Yeo been thinking when he'd involved Jennifer Armitage in all this! Richard knew that he needed to contain this quickly.

'Say nothing to anyone about this. You hear me?' He had stopped walking and had forcefully grabbed Jennifer by the shoulders to turn her towards him.

Fortunately for Richard, they were at the quieter end of Edward Street, and the lunchtime rush had not yet commenced. The discussion was over. He left Jennifer still shaking on the sidewalk.

Black reflected on how hard he had worked to reach this level, and the risks he'd taken along the way. He'd skipped university and had travelled extensively throughout Asia. He was always pushing the envelope and it was this attribute that had caught the attention of George Kim. Richard had started working for Kim in the property development industry in Hong Kong in his late twenties. He had been lucky and had successfully overseen several large hotel and commercial developments in Hong Kong and Malaysia. At Kim's suggestion, Richard had returned to Australia five years ago with excellent credentials to take up the position of Chief Operating Officer at Pacific Property. Now in his late thirties Black had recently progressed to replace the outgoing CEO at Pacific, whose ill health had precipitated her retirement. And no one was going to stop his upward trajectory.

Chapter 22

Back at his desk, Jackson dialled Jason Jones' number.

'How'd it go, mate?' was Jones' prompt answer.

'The plot thickens,' replied Jackson. 'There were some very interesting reactions to the report around the boardroom table. I'm beginning to see Peter Tomlinson as just a shit stirrer. You know, one of those "difficult for the sake of being difficult" members every board needs to ensure the contrary view is always present in the debate. Shaun Ingram and Kevin Lightfoot look to be both playing a straight bat, and I'm pretty sure Ros Green is not involved. Jennifer Armitage and Richard Black are, however, a whole different kettle of fish.'

'How so?'

'Jennifer looked to be quite distraught at the possible connection of HK Investments with owners of casinos in Macau. A bit strange really. On the face of it, that would not appear to be anything, at least not yet, that an individual director should fear. She is certainly involved, although I'm not sure to what extent. Richard Black, on the other hand, looks to be up to his armpits in it. He positively goaded Jennifer, and she was visibly shaken by what was said.'

Jones did not ask him to elaborate. He didn't need to as Tom was keen to continue.

'I took a bit of a calculated risk in a separate subsequent meeting with just Ros Green and Richard Black. I mentioned the rumours about the massive gambling debt owed by James Yeo to what I said may well be an illegal casino in Hong Kong.'

'Fuck, mate. That's a big risk. If we're right about this, there's a lot at stake here. I'd be very careful from now on. How did that go down?'

Jason seemed a bit surprised that Jackson had done this, although he had known him for long enough to be aware that Jackson's instincts were usually very sound and rarely let him down.

'Well, Richard didn't take that too well. In fact, as I had observed a couple of times during the board meeting, he completely lost his composure and became very aggressive. I'm sure that I hit a real nerve. Black reacted as though he may have some proprietorial interest in the outcome of the deal, other than, of course, that which he clearly has in his capacity as CEO of Pacific.'

'So where to from here?' Jason was not one to waste words.

Jackson continued. 'I'm to ask you to investigate both ownership and funding sources over the next twenty-four hours, and then prepare a further and final report for the board on any new findings.'

'Roger that, mate. Not a lot of time, but I'll see what I can turn up. Can I suggest that I prepare two reports? One with only verifiable facts, and a supplementary one that draws together all of the other information and surrounding circumstances for distribution to a more limited audience.'

Jackson thought about that for a minute. 'Maybe not, Jason. It could be dangerous to put that in print. I'm meeting with Ros Green tonight at 6:30 p.m., and I'll run the concept by her. In the meantime, see if you can make any progress on either front before that meeting, please.'

'Roger that.' The call had ended.

Jackson thought of updating Max Grenfell on the latest, but decided not to. While Max always made time for Jackson, he had a very busy practice and usually had to put something aside to do so. In any event, Tom saw that Max's light on his frequent contact list was white, meaning that Max's computer and phone had been inactive for over an hour. He was most likely out of the office.

He decided instead to head to the nearby botanic gardens in Alice Street to clear his head. As he left his office and headed towards the lift, he was almost mowed down by Frederick Anderson, the managing partner of Ridgeway's Mason's Brisbane office.

Frederick had only recently been appointed to the position, and his personality had immediately changed. For some reason when given a little power, many lawyers allowed that to go to their heads and took on an elevated level of self-importance.

Frederick was no different. He had taken to walking briskly around the narrow corridors of the firm, and more often than not directly at you, presumably with the expectation that lesser mortals would quickly get out of his way. That hadn't worked with Jackson, and that may be one of the reasons why Jackson had found himself on the outer lately.

Over the years, the lawyer had observed that most of his partners simply took the path of least resistance and complied with whatever management, local or national, required. *Whatever happened to good old-fashioned integrity?* He mused to himself as he left the building. *When had individual financial reward become so important?* But he knew the answer was: since always.

Chapter 23

Richard Black decided to breach agreed protocol and dialled George Kim's direct line. He knew Kim would be contacting him later in the day, but he wanted to update the man on the latest developments and alert him to his concerns that Jennifer Armitage may be unravelling.

Kim sounded surprised to hear Richard's voice. 'I assume this is about the board meeting at Pacific this morning?'

'Correct,' said Richard, and he quickly continued. 'I think we have a problem with Jennifer Armitage. She looks to be unravelling, and I have a concern that she plans to discuss this in more detail this evening with her partner, Ian Fox. Ian is a highly respected forensic investigation accountant in the Brisbane office of a global accounting firm. Of equal concern is the fact that Jackson's investigator's report made a link to our other Cayman entity, although at this stage the connection is tenuous at best.

'On top of that, I met with Ros Green and Jackson after the meeting, and Jackson told me that his investigator has uncovered rumours about a possible massive gambling debt owed by James Yeo to an illegal casino in Hong Kong. This is all starting to close in a little.'

Richard heard an audible intake of breath from George Kim when he mentioned Yeo's possible gambling debt.

'We need to shut this down.' Kim exhaled loudly as he spoke. 'We've all worked too hard to get to this point.'

'Agreed,' said Richard patiently. He wanted to remind Kim once again that he had on more than one occasion urged the syndicate to break the $750 million into smaller parcels so as not to draw too much attention. The majority had, however, agreed that the planets seemed to have aligned, and that they had sufficient contacts and controls in place to steer this through in one deal. Richard was eventually persuaded to this view, accepting that the confluence of events that had resulted in the huge gambling debt owed to the syndicate by Yeo, at this particular time, was a one-off opportunity.

But perhaps they had made an error in making the deal too sweet for Pacific, mistakenly believing that it would be grabbed by the board with both hands, and without question. No one had anticipated the level of investigation that had ensued. He had erroneously not allowed for Tom Jackson. Returning to the present, he asked George Kim what he had in mind.

Refocusing, Kim continued. 'I'll call Yeo and tell him that he should not have any more direct contact with Jennifer, simply on the basis that the arrangement is no longer of any use. I also think we should convince Jennifer that it would be unwise to discuss this further with anyone.'

Richard agreed, but reminded Kim that Jennifer was likely to discuss this further with her partner, Ian Fox, that evening.

'I have something in mind that will cover that possibility, and at the same time send an unequivocal message to Jennifer.'

There was a sinister tone to Kim's voice. Richard thought it best not to enquire into what he had in mind, and the man's silence confirmed that he too was of the view that it was best Richard not have this information.

They agreed to make contact again the following day.

Chapter 24

George Kim's first call was to James Yeo. 'I want you to make no further direct contact with Jennifer Armitage.'

No explanation was given, and none requested. Nothing further was said. Kim was aware that Yeo knew better than to rock this particular boat. He was between a rock and a hard place, and desperately needed this deal to proceed to a successful conclusion.

Next, he called Murray Jensen in London on his secure line. It was Kim who had introduced James Yeo to Jensen a couple of years ago. Murray was the 'go-to' person for challenging, and more often than not, completely illegal assignments anywhere in the world. It was very early in the morning in London, but neither Jensen nor Kim would think anything of this. The exorbitant retainers that Jensen deservedly commanded allowed for 24/7 access.

'It's George Kim, Murray. I need your further involvement in a matter you're already connected with in Brisbane, Australia.'

'Happy to oblige,' was Jensen's expected response.

'How good is your asset in Brisbane?'

'The best.'

Kim quickly told Murray what he required, and provided all relevant details. There was no need for them to discuss a fee arrangement. Kim and his colleagues were among Jensen's best repeat clientele, and each knew what the expectations of the other were.

*

'You're in luck, Sarina.' Jensen began the call to her with an almost condescending tone, knowing that this would get her attention immediately. 'You have a perfect opportunity to prove to me and our important clients exactly what you're capable of.'

He proceeded to explain to Sarina George what was required and emphasised to her that time was of the essence.

'I will not let you down,' was all she said.

Chapter 25

Jackson had not yet had a chance to catch up with Max Grenfell. He was contemplating doing so when his phone rang. It was Jason Jones.

'Jason. Thanks for getting back to me before my meeting with Ros this evening. Anything new?'

'Sweet FA, mate,' was Jason's typically short response. 'Every which way I turn ends up being another dry gully.'

'Okay then. I'll see what Ros says about your second report concept, but I expect she'll agree with me that it's best such a report does not exist. I'll let you know if she thinks otherwise. Find out what you can by midday tomorrow please, and finalise your report.'

'Roger that,' was Jason's customary sign off.

Jackson headed to the Black Stump pub in Albert Street. It was 6:20 p.m., and he knew it would take him about ten minutes to walk there. He did not want to be late for his meeting with Ros. On the way to the pub, he reflected on his attraction to her, and his mind wandered to a conference two years ago when the two of them had drunk a little too much and had almost slept together.

The Black Stump pub had been a good choice for his meeting with Ros. It usually hummed on a Thursday night, but not until much later. At this time of the evening, there was no loud music, and the small number of drinkers generated only a low conversational hum. He found Ros sitting in a booth towards the rear of the venue, where the lighting was dimmer. The booths on either side were not occupied.

'Right on time, as usual,' Ros greeted Jackson with a suggestive smile. 'The ice cold Peroni Legerra has only just arrived.'

Jackson did not drink a lot of beer but when he did, the Perroni Leggera was his favourite. *How nice of Ros to remember that.*

Ros mischievously patted the seat beside her. He had been able to resist in the past but this time he relented and slid in to her side of the booth. Tom found it difficult to look away from her sparkling green eyes.

'How are you dealing with your newfound freedom?' Tom was aware that Ros' divorce had recently been finalised.

Ros turned to face Jackson, and their knees rubbed together under the table. Tom involuntarily flinched and moved his knee away, quickly returning it when he realised what he'd done.

'Happy and free to do whatever and whomever I like.' Ros put her hand on his knee playfully.

Jackson looked deeply into her eyes and a warm smile slowly made its way across his face. God, she was sexy. But he turned the conversation back towards business.

'Nothing new from Jason Jones.' Jackson had noticed that the pub was starting to fill up, and thought it best to get the meeting back on track.

They both sat up a little straighter, but their knees remained touching and Ros did not remove her hand.

'He'll keep investigating and will give me his final report around midday tomorrow, although he continues to hit brick walls and is not expecting to turn up anything new within that very limited time frame. He did suggest, however, that he produce a second report for more limited circulation, which details all of the additional and as yet unverified information he has available.' Tom knew that would include his traffic incident and Mary's coincidental experience yesterday. He didn't want to discuss anything about Mary with Ros though.

'I think it would be a mistake to produce a second report comprised of rumours and suspected coincidences,' Ros said thoughtfully. 'I think you've already gone out on a limb raising the rumoured gambling debt with Richard after today's board meeting. I mentioned that I've had concerns about this deal from the outset. I am now almost certain that Richard Black is involved somehow, and I don't like it. It is such a great deal for the company, however, so I don't want to dismiss it lightly. That said, if we are able to prove illegal activity with any certainty, the deal will be off, and I will be the first to go to the authorities.'

They talked for some time about the alternative courses of action available to them, assuming for the purposes of the discussion that Jason Jones did not turn up any additional information. They both felt the need to become directly involved, although each came to that conclusion with some trepidation.

There was too much at stake here to involve others, and, in any event, they were unsure of who they could trust. It was critical that they quickly resolve this, one way or the other.

They weren't sure initially if they should head to Hong Kong themselves to confront the board and management of HK Investments, or if they should go to London to further investigate the possible link between the two Cayman Island entities. Either way, they concluded that direct action was necessary.

A consensus was reached that they head to London as quickly as possible.

Jackson's concern about his and Ros' deeper involvement in the shadier aspects of the deal was offset a little by the thought of spending more time with her. 'I'll have a chat with Jason to get his thoughts on this, and also to get him to assist with setting up some meetings in London. We could head off on Saturday, hold meetings on Monday and Tuesday, and be back in Brisbane by Thursday at the latest.'

They finished their drinks while chatting about their mutual interest in travelling. With some obvious reluctance, they slid out of the booth and headed off in separate directions.

Chapter 26

Jennifer Armitage was almost hysterical by the time she arrived home. But after a couple of glasses of red wine, she was far more composed by the time her partner, Ian Fox, got home later in the evening.

'I'm not sure what I've gotten myself into,' she sobbed as she fell into Ian's arms.

'Whoa, what's up?' asked Ian, his brows knitting together in concern.

'It has to do with my directorship at Pacific Property. I told you how that came about, and at the time I said I was a little surprised, but felt that my luck had finally changed. What I haven't told you about is a call I received from James Yeo, a heavy hitter in the global property industry, not long after my appointment.'

Jennifer proceeded to unload everything, pausing only momentarily from time to time to take a deep breath and another sip of her red wine. By the time she'd finished, her glass was empty again, and she slumped back in her seat.

Ian sat still for a while, absorbing everything Jennifer had just said. He calmly asked some further questions, and Jennifer responded as best as she could. He needed have as much information as she had available so he could effectively analyse it. That's how his mind worked.

'I have a road trip to Warwick and Toowoomba tomorrow, which I can't put off.' Ian took her hands in his. 'It's a round trip, so I'll have to leave early. I have a couple of ideas about all this, and will discreetly set a few lines of enquiry in motion before I head off.'

Jennifer wanted to protest and prevent Ian's involvement. She knew he was busy, and, more importantly, thought that he may be putting himself in some sort of danger by helping her. She was, however, so upset, and her thought processes numbed by good red wine that she simply thanked her partner, feeling that at least some of the weight had been lifted off her shoulders.

Chapter 27

DAY 5 (Friday)

Ian Fox was a brilliant investigative accountant. He had made partner at his firm well ahead of his contemporaries. Now in his mid-thirties, Ian was slightly built and a little under six feet tall, with delicate hands. His short, straight brown hair accentuated his long face. In stark contrast to his almost effeminate appearance, he had a very strong personality and was highly intelligent and quick-witted.

Fox was deeply in love with Jennifer Armitage and was extremely concerned at the state she'd been in the previous evening. He felt he had no choice but to assist her with her dilemma. Ian knew his way around global money laundering conspiracies and had concluded that this was most likely what Jennifer may have become mixed up in.

Fox arrived at his office at 6 a.m. and quickly made contact with two of his trusted European colleagues he knew would still be in the office. One was a partner in their London office, and the other a trusted investigator based in London. He gave each a precis of the detail he had available and emphasised the need for absolute secrecy and discretion. He was confident that, if anything was amiss, one of these two would be able to uncover it.

Having initiated these lines of enquiry, Ian felt a little more relieved. He gathered his file and other reference material for his meetings today in Warwick and Toowoomba and headed to the basement of his building in the Brisbane CBD. As he left the carpark in his white Porsche

911 Carrera, he failed to notice the silver AMG Mercedes leave the kerb and follow him at a distance.

Fox loved driving his Porsche, and was particularly excited about today's trip. He had a lot of territory to cover in one day, but a trip on the Cunningham Highway through the Main Range National Park was one of his favourite drives. It was a route he had taken on multiple occasions since he purchased the Porsche eighteen months ago.

Chapter 28

Sarina George couldn't believe her luck when Jensen had offered her a position in his operation shortly after her dishonourable discharge from the British army almost two years ago. She didn't need to know how Jensen came to contact her. All that mattered was that she had fallen on her feet in a role that allowed her to unleash her dark side.

Sarina instinctively knew that Murray Jensen had presented her with a career-defining opportunity. She was so excited, and knew that she would not be able to sleep. Sarina wasn't sure how she would go about accomplishing the task set for her, but didn't want to miss any chance to do so. She had staked out Ian Fox's apartment in Paddington shortly after midnight.

A little surprised at his early departure, Sarina was glad that she'd affixed a well-hidden micro tracking device under the rear of his car. There was hardly any traffic on the roads at that time of the morning, and he would surely have noticed that she was following him.

As Fox drove out of the basement, Sarina followed not long after but stayed well out of sight. She kept a close eye on the screen of her iPhone, which she had linked to the sophisticated tracking device via satellite. It wasn't long before she realised that Ian was heading west, away from Brisbane. To her delight, he turned in a south-westerly direction from Ipswich and headed onto the Cunningham Highway, towards Warwick. She felt she needed to move closer to his Porsche so that he would not get too far ahead.

Sarina had also driven this road many times before, and knew now what she had to do. Cunningham's Gap in Main Range National Park on the Cunningham Highway, was a notorious black spot for traffic accidents.

She'd been progressively closing the gap between hers and Ian's car. She had noticed him looking in the rearview mirror, and thought she had seen him issue a 'thumbs-up' challenge to her, immediately before his car rapidly accelerated into the now sharper twists and turns on the highway.

Perfect, she thought to herself. Sarina had undergone several intensive driver training courses, and knew that she would easily have Ian's measure, no matter how good he was. She also knew exactly where to close in.

As they approached the part of the highway she had mentally selected, Sarina planted her foot. The worked engine in the AMG responded, and she easily caught Ian's Porsche. She was close enough now the see the look of surprise and panic on his face in her target's rearview mirror, just before contact.

They were travelling at 150 kilometres per hour and the sudden impact to the rear of Ian's vehicle caused him to lose control immediately. His Porsche careened off the side of the road and into a huge eucalyptus tree at the start of a heavily wooded area.

Even though the impact between the cars had only been slight, the high speed had amplified the effect, and Sarina had to fight to gain control of her car. Her training kicked in, and she regained control and slowed to a more sensible speed.

Sarina couldn't believe her luck. From what she had been able to observe in her rearview mirror, while fighting to regain control of her AMG, she was certain that Ian had not survived. His Porsche had hit the massive tree dead centre, and the car looked to have almost disintegrated on impact.

As it was still early, Sarina had only seen a couple of other cars on the highway. She was relieved that, as she drove on at a more sedate 100 kilometres per hour, she did not spot another car coming in the opposite direction for a further ten kilometres or so.

Thinking quickly, and certain that she'd achieved what she had set out to, Sarina decided to continue on to Warwick, from where she would contact Jensen via secure satellite link.

'It's done,' was all she needed to say to Murray Jensen. Even though it was quite late in London, Jensen was still awake, and delighted to receive the news.

'Are you certain?'

'Yes. Have a look at traffic reports west of Brisbane over the next hour or so,' said Sarina confidently as she terminated the call, feeling very pleased with herself.

Sarina treated herself to a late breakfast in a café in the main street of Warwick. It was a café she had visited before, and she recalled being pleasantly surprised at the level of quality of the food and coffee. After a delicious breakfast and a second coffee, she opened the website for Queensland traffic at the Department of Transport and Main Roads. She keyed in the Cunningham Highway and saw that it was closed due to a single-vehicle collision at Cunningham's Gap, which had resulted in a fatality. Sarina inwardly grinned to herself.

Knowing that the traffic accident investigators may take some time to try and piece things together, and that the highway would remain closed while they investigated, Sarina decided to find an alternative route back to Brisbane.

She thought momentarily about the micro tracking device she'd attached to Ian's car. Even if they did locate it, and that was highly unlikely given the speed at impact and the dense undergrowth she'd observed, there was no way it could be traced to her. The device was readily available online and in electronics stores. She had paid cash for two such devices over twelve months ago, reasoning that she may need them some day, and she'd worn latex gloves when affixing the device to Ian Fox's car. Once she'd terminated the satellite link between the device and her phone, she knew that it was not possible to identify from the device what that link had been.

Chapter 29

As was customary, Jackson checked his office on arrival, something he did slightly more thoroughly these days, to see that everything was as he'd left it the day before. He was relieved to see that it was, and, so far as he could tell, he had again not been followed by the silver AMG Mercedes on the way in this morning.

Focus, Tom, he reminded himself. *This is a long way from being over, and there's a lot to do.*

First, he had to call Ros Green. As he did so, he mentally weighed the pros and cons of what lay ahead of them. They were both going out on a limb by heading to London, although time alone with Ros on the other side of the world had its own appeals.

She answered immediately. 'Tom, I'm still keen to head to London. And you?' They had both agreed to think about it further overnight.

'Yes,' replied Jackson. 'I'll have my PA book the business class flights to London, leaving tomorrow and returning on Thursday.'

'Good idea. I'll have the company reimburse your firm. Just include it as a disbursement on your next bill.'

While this was a little unusual, Jackson readily agreed in the circumstances. Speed was of the essence. 'Will you need to get CEO approval for the expenditure, Ros?'

'Yes, I will. I've been thinking about it this morning. The best thing for me to do is address that directly with Richard today. What can he say? He knows how important this deal is, and also that it's critical we put to rest any suggestion that criminal elements may be involved. Document negotiation can continue while we're away. If he protests and tries to stop me from going with you, we will know with more certainty that he's likely to be complicit in an illegality.'

'Good luck with that, and be careful please.' There was genuine concern in Jackson's voice. He knew they were doing what they had to, but that didn't make it any easier. 'I'll have a chat to Jason Jones shortly to see if he has anything further, and to get him to set up meetings with his contacts, and with the London agent for the Cayman entities on Monday and Tuesday in London. I'll call you later with the details, and in the meantime, let me know how you get on with Richard.'

'Will do,' Ros responded in a tone that Tom thought to be more playful than businesslike. 'I'm looking forward to a productive and meaningful trip.'

Jackson's executive assistant, Samantha Brown, had arrived while he was on the phone. She was usually early, particularly when she was aware that Jackson had plenty on.

'Morning, Sam,' Jackson greeted her. They had a great working relationship. Samantha had been his assistant for the past five years. She took pride in her work, and was happy that Jackson made her feel an integral part of his team's success. 'I need you to book Ros Green and me on flights to London tomorrow, please, returning to Brisbane by next Thursday.'

'Business class, I assume, and which file do I charge?' Sam replied pleasantly.

'Yes please, and charge it to the Pacific Property–HK Investments file. I'll show Ros' airfare as a disbursement on the next bill, which is due to go out next week.'

'On to it straight away,' beamed Sam, as she spun around in her chair and began tapping at the keys on her keyboard.

Samantha was in her early thirties and was so efficient that Tom often thought of her as another pair of hands. She was attractive with long dark hair and a well-proportioned plus-size physique. On more than one occasion, Jackson had had to resist Sam's seductive advances at work functions. He was well aware that relationships at work were not advisable, but that's not to say that he hadn't been tempted from time to time.

Tom decided to call Jason Jones before he brought Max Grenfell up to speed. He hadn't yet had an opportunity to speak to Max after yesterday's board meeting.

'Did you wet the bed again, mate?' was Jason's crude way of commenting on the early hour of Jackson's call.

'Morning, Jason. Anything new?'

'Fucking dry gullies in every direction, accompanied by much silence and ever-increasing levels of unavailability. I think we have all we're gonna get, but I'll bat on for another couple of hours.'

Jackson thanked Jones and told him of the plan for he and Ros to head to London tomorrow, and the reasons why.

'Shit, Tom. I understand why you want to do that, but I think that's way too far above and beyond the call. You guys are taking a helluva risk. I hear ya though, and know just who you should meet. My key contacts, of course, and there's a guy at Mathers Crompton, the law firm that acts as the London agent for numerous Cayman entities. I've spoken to him a couple of times. Good bloke, and I get the feeling that he knows a lot more than he's prepared to say over the phone, even though I thought at one stage he was about to spill the beans. His name's Arthur Derwent. I'll set up meetings on Monday or Tuesday.'

'Thanks, Jason. I owe you big time on this one.'

'Just come back in one piece, mate. And Tom?'

'Yes?'

'It's fuckin' cold over there. Could freeze the balls off a brass monkey.'

Jackson smiled at Jason's profanity then thanked him for the excellent work he'd done for them on short notice. Jason said he'd email details of the meetings to Jackson's private email address, just as a precaution. Tom had told Jason about the enemy within.

Next Jackson called Max, just to make sure he had the time available for a comprehensive update. He could really use Max's wise input on this. Max was free, and Jackson went straight to his office and closed the door before he sat down.

'This really is moving fast,' began Jackson.

Max remained silent so Jackson could continue. Tom could tell by his expression that he was worried about the position his good friend had found himself in.

Jackson took Max through yesterday's board meeting, the meeting with Ros and Richard afterwards, his subsequent meeting with Ros, and his various chats with Jason Jones.

'I agree, no second report,' said Max, after taking a little time to consider the latest revelations from Jackson. 'London, eh? Are you certain you want to immerse yourself in this that deeply?'

Jackson nodded assuredly.

'Have you seen the news feeds this morning?' continued Max.

'I've been on the phone for a while. Anything in particular?' Jackson inclined his head, not knowing what to expect.

'Ian Fox, from global accounting firm Braxton Bartholemew, was killed in a horrific single-vehicle accident at Cunningham's Gap this morning. They reckon his Porsche must have been travelling at 140k-plus through the S bends. Had to pretty much scrape him off a gum tree. His car was unrecognisable. It may just be a coincidence, but isn't he Jennifer Armitage's partner?'

Jackson knew that, and he was more than shocked at this news. He silently contemplated the disturbing news, clenching his fists until his knuckles turned white. He felt the need to lash out and punch or kick something or someone. Gathering his thoughts, he wondered out loud, 'Maybe a coincidence?' but he didn't believe that, and he could see that Max didn't either.

Chapter 30

'Bingo,' Miles Fletcher said to himself. His obsessive checking of Jackson's Pacific Property file had paid off again. He rushed around to Roger Everingham's office, and was pleased to see that Roger was not on the phone this time. The lazy bastard still had his feet on the desk though.

Miles ignored Everingham's feet on the desk and his general slovenly appearance. 'Jackson's PA has just requisitioned the firm's travel agent to book business class flights for he and Ros Green to London tomorrow, returning Thursday.'

Roger flopped his feet off his desk, grinned at Miles and picked up his phone as he dialled. 'Thanks, Miles. Fascinating. Shut the door on your way out.'

*

James Yeo's response was more pleasant than it had been two days ago. 'Roger. What's new?'

'Jackson and Ros Green are off to London tomorrow, returning on Thursday,' Roger eagerly blurted out.

'Are you certain?' Yeo queried.

'Absolutely.'

Roger waited for James to continue, but he had hung up. Everingham had no idea of the significance of the information, but that didn't stop him from congratulating himself once again.

*

James Yeo had dialled George Kim's number immediately to pass on this information.

'Thanks, James. Very helpful.' Kim needed to get this information to Richard Black quickly, so he terminated the call with Yeo and dialled Richard's number.

'Did you know Tom Jackson and Ros Green plan to head to London tomorrow?' Kim began as soon as the CEO answered the phone.

Richard was silent for a moment before responding. 'No. They must have only decided that overnight.'

They both knew why a trip to London could be considered necessary, but neither could understand why Jackson and Green had decided to involve themselves personally in this.

'Ros Green will need my approval for the trip expenditure, so I expect she'll be in to see me this morning,' Richard continued.

They discussed how best to proceed. Both came to the conclusion that Richard had no alternative other than to approve the expenditure. To do otherwise might be regarded as suspicious. They also agreed that George Kim should speak to Murray Jensen in London.

Chapter 31

'Not long after Richard put the phone down, Ros Green was standing in the doorway to his office.

'Have you got a minute?' Ros said pleasantly. She thought Richard seemed a little more relaxed this morning, but then again, he had always been very good at hiding his emotions, until recently.

'Sure, close the door and come in.'

Ros and Tom had discussed how best to raise this with Richard. The logic of why the travel was necessary was undeniable. Ros eloquently took Richard through her arguments in support of the trip. Richard, of course, already knew all of the information that she was presenting to him. Nonetheless, Ros thought it necessary and appropriate that she collate it in the context of her proposal.

Ros concluded. 'I expect that, by the end of next week, final documents will have been agreed, and we will have hopefully been able to allay any fears about the bona fides of all components of the transaction. The board can then make an informed decision about how it wishes to proceed.'

'That all makes sense. It's a shame the meetings can't be held remotely, but I understand face-to-face meetings can be more beneficial in circumstances such as these. I respect your judgement on this, Ros. Go ahead, and please keep me posted as things develop.'

That was much too easy, Ros thought to herself. She had been expecting some sort of counter-argument from Richard. It would not be an inexpensive exercise, although she reasoned to herself that, like her, Richard saw the deal as being hugely beneficial to Pacific, and he was also committed to it proceeding.

Chapter 32

Like most people these days, Jennifer Armitage received news alerts on her smartphone throughout the day. She usually scanned the story, then quickly deleted it.

Today was very different. The news alert was headed: 'A Horrific Single-Vehicle Accident at Cunningham's Gap Has Closed the Cunningham Highway.' First responders have described the almost unrecognisable wreck of the Porsche, commenting that very high speed must have been involved in the fatal accident...'

Jennifer almost dropped her phone. *Surely that's not Ian. It can't be.* Almost at the same time as she lowered her head to her hands, her mobile rang. There was no caller ID. She almost didn't take the call. It was the police, confirming her worst fears. It was Ian.

What on earth had happened? What had he been thinking? A wave of emotions consumed her. She was angry at first, profoundly sad, and finally fearful.

As she collected her thoughts, she began to wonder if the accident may not have been an accident after all. Was it an unfortunate coincidence, or did it have something to do with what they had discussed the night before?

Jennifer decided to call Ian's closest friend and colleague in Braxton Bartholemew, Ray Kean. 'Have you heard the terrible news, Ray?' she sobbed into the phone.

'I have, and I can't believe it. I'm so sorry, Jennifer. Please let me know if there's anything I can do for you. He will be a huge loss to many.'

Ray was a good friend. He and his wife Katrina had been to Jennifer and Ian's place on many occasions.

Through tears, Jennifer managed to say, 'This may not have been an accident.'

'All reports I've seen suggest that it was a single-vehicle accident,' said Ray quickly, not wanting Jennifer to contemplate the horrible details any longer than was necessary. 'You've been in the car with Ian numerous times, as have I, and we both know he regularly pushed it to the limits, and sometimes beyond.'

Jennifer knew that Ray was right. *Maybe it was just an accident*, she wailed inwardly. Almost as an afterthought, she asked if Ian had been in the office before he'd headed west.

'I believe so, but not for long. Why do you ask?'

Jennifer hesitated momentarily. 'We discussed something highly sensitive and confidential last night, and he had planned to make some enquiries to see if he could assist.' She was still wiping tears away, but was starting to think more clearly now.

'As you know, we're both in the Forensic Investigation Division, and we've worked very closely together for many years now. It shouldn't take me long to find out if Ian initiated anything when he was in the office this morning,' responded Ray, helpfully.

After the call had ended, Jennifer wondered if she should have mentioned anything to Ray. *It's done now*, she thought. *Best to wait and see if Ray turns up anything.*

Chapter 33

The final report from JJ Investigations arrived in Jackson's inbox a little before midday. Jackson saw that it did not contain anything new. It was the same report he had presented at the Pacific board meeting the day before. Tom was relieved to see that Jason had not made mention of any details relating to his and Ros' trip to London.

He checked his private email address, and saw that, true to his word, Jason had arranged for Jackson and Ros to meet with two of Jason's key contacts on Monday afternoon in London. He had also been able to arrange for them to meet with Arthur Derwent at Mathers Crompton on the Tuesday. That was good news, and of itself made the trip worthwhile.

Jackson called Ros to let her know arrangements had been made for the travel, and meetings on Monday and Tuesday. 'How did you go with Richard?'

'I gave a very polished performance, even if I do say so myself,' Ros replied. 'Richard approved the expenditure, but it was a bit too easy. As we discussed, if he's a crook, he didn't really have a choice. If he's not, then he would be happy that the trip offers an opportunity to bring things to a head quickly. We all want this deal to proceed, Tom.'

Chapter 34

DAY 6 (Saturday)

Jackson had plenty of time to pack on the Saturday. The flight was not leaving until 10 p.m. that evening from Brisbane International Airport. It was a direct flight to Tokyo, with a three-hour stopover, and then on to London, arriving at 1 p.m. Sunday, London time. Jackson always enjoyed a stopover in Japan. The Japanese did things differently. They took such pride in all aspects of everyday life.

His assistant Samantha had provided he and Ros with a detailed itinerary and checklist. He was interested to see that they were flying on one of Qantas' new A380 airbuses. Tom and Ros had been allocated business class seats towards the front of the upper deck, adjacent to each other.

Jackson loved to fly on the A380. His first flight on one was when he and Mary had travelled to London for the 2012 Olympics, with Malaysia Airlines. The plane was so new it still had plastic on some of the seats. That was before two subsequent very high-profile unfortunate accidents involving Malaysia Airlines flights MH17 and MH370. He reflected briefly again on what the passengers must have gone through and hoped they had not suffered too much. Tom had a mild fear of flying, but oddly enough found comfort in the fact that, if there was an accident, it would all be over fairly quickly.

Turning his mind to happier thoughts, Jackson decided to head out for a relaxed brunch at one of the many nearby cafes. He briefly thought about how often he and Mary had done just that, and again found himself wondering whether he could salvage his marriage. Would she ever forgive him for sleeping with one of the senior lawyers at another firm? *Why did I even tell her about it?* But with their busy schedules, they'd barely had time for each other before his indiscretions, and had not slept together for months. It was no excuse, Tom knew, but the temptation had just been too much to resist.

Chapter 35

Ray Kean called Jennifer Armitage around 10 a.m. on Saturday morning. 'How are you doing, Jen? I know this must be an awful time for you.'

'Not great,' Jennifer replied. She sounded terrible. 'I didn't get a lot of sleep last night. The police came around in the evening to talk about Ian's accident. You always see in the movies that the distraught widow is taken to the morgue to identify the body. Not this time, Ray. There was not much left to identify. They said they'd had to identify Ian from his dental records.'

Ray gasped on the other end of the line. 'Oh Jen, I'm so sorry. Would you like Katrina and me to come around and keep you company, or do you need some time on your own?'

'I need company, please,' said Jennifer, tears welling up again.

'We'll be there in twenty minutes, with a coffee and some croissants,' Ray said sympathetically. They lived in the neighbouring suburb of Bardon, and Ray planned to drop into a local favourite French bakery on the way over.

Jennifer quickly showered so she did not look such a mess when they arrived. There was not much she could do about her red eyes. She had been sobbing most of the night, wondering if she may have had something to do with Ian's death.

Ray and Katrina arrived with piping hot coffee and warm croissants. 'Life savers. Thankyou.' Jennifer greeted them at the door to her apartment.

After doing their best to exchange pleasantries while they polished off the coffee and croissants, Jennifer felt the need to satisfy her curiosity. 'Did you find anything?'

Ray knew what she was referring to. 'Yes. Ian is, was, sorry, an extremely efficient operator. Before he headed off yesterday, he made two calls, one to a partner in our London office, and another to an investigator in London we have both instructed in the past. I managed to speak to each of them very early this morning, before they left the office for the day, Friday their time. They had both heard about Ian's unfortunate accident and had commented on the coincidental timing. I had to be quite insistent, but eventually they each told me what Ian had asked them to investigate for him. Bloody hell, Jen! What's this all about?'

Jennifer slumped into her chair, but managed to hold her emotions in check, for now. She told them both the whole story, starting with her appointment to the Pacific board six months ago, and ending with a description of the distraught state she had been in when Ian came home two nights ago. Neither Ray nor Katrina said anything to interrupt Jennifer's story. They both sat motionless, looking at her incredulously.

'I'm not sure about you two, but I for one don't believe in coincidence,' Ray finally said after a prolonged period of silence, except for the sound of Jennifer's weeping. Jennifer and Katrina nodded in unison. 'Would you like me to give our London contacts the go-ahead to continue with the work Ian asked them to undertake?'

Jennifer looked terrified all of a sudden. 'Are you sure that's a good idea?' she whispered.

'I think we owe it to Ian, don't you?' was all Ray needed to say.

The three of them agreed that they would tell no one of their plans. It would be only Ray who had direct, and then only verbal, contact with the two contacts in London. They agreed to reconvene as soon as Ray had heard anything further.

Chapter 36

Even though it was the weekend, Miles Fletcher was in the office early in the morning. He worked most Saturdays, as did many in the firm. He had arrived a little earlier than usual today so that he could pursue his new obsession of uncovering confidential information about Jackson's current activities.

They were all partners, weren't they? he reasoned. *What's the harm in tracking the activity of a fellow partner.* After all, they were each liable for the other's actions.

Fletcher was devious at best, but, even for him, what he was about to do was certainly pushing the limits. He opened his laptop, hit 'switch user' and typed in Samantha Brown's name. Samantha had proven to be an exceptional personal assistant to Jackson, but she was very predictable, allowing Miles to guess her login password with ease. *Who would use their oft-talked about pet's name as a sensitive password?* Miles thought to himself.

As the screen came to life, he was acutely aware that he should not linger too long. He quickly saw that, as expected, Jackson had provided delegated authority for Samantha to access his work emails. He knew that Jackson had a very short list of persons he trusted, but had been confident that Samantha would be on it. What he hadn't expected, however, and what proved to be an absolute bonus, was that Jackson had also provided delegated access to his private Gmail address.

Tom Jackson was extremely careful and took great care in limiting those who had access to his information. What he had failed to consider was the reprehensible behaviour someone like Miles Fletcher might stoop to. After all, how does one counter blatant dishonesty in a collective of business proprietors whose success depends on an inherent trust of each other?

Working quickly, Miles was able to search for, and separate, all emails on Jackson's work and private email accounts that related to the Pacific Property matter. An email from Jason Jones of JJ Investigations to Jackson on his private email yesterday drew his attention. *This is absolute gold*, he thought, almost salivating at the discovery. He quickly made a written note of the meetings that Jones had arranged for Jackson and Ros Green in London this coming Monday and Tuesday, and logged out of Samantha's site. He wondered briefly if the footprint of his intrusion would be discoverable.

Fletcher checked that the adjoining offices and work areas were still deserted, and dialled Roger Everingham's number. He knew Roger to be lazy. He never came in to the office on the weekend. That said, he hadn't expected him to sound sleepy at that time of the morning.

'What is it, mate?' yawned Roger. He quickly became more alert as Miles began describing the results of his sleuthing activities.

'Fucking jackpot, Miles. Fascinating. I need to pass this on quickly. Thanks again, eh.'

*

It was still early in Hong Kong, but James Yeo answered Roger Everingham's call on the first ring. He was interested in any new information at almost any hour of the day, and Yeo wasted no time in relaying it to George Kim. Yeo was, however, becoming increasingly concerned about precisely what he may have become involved in. He knew he had to go along with whatever it was, for now. He had no choice.

Now in his late forties, James had studied economics in Hong Kong and had very early in his career decided that he had a passion and aptitude for numbers. Living in one of the largest financial centres in the world, he'd fallen into a career in finance. Yeo had worked hard for his successes, and his career had been on a steep trajectory from the moment he'd left university in his early twenties. *Why have I put all that at risk?* He inwardly cursed himself.

*

George Kim realised that this was getting a little too close for comfort. He didn't know Arthur Derwent, but was almost certain that no one at Mathers Crompton would divulge any highly confidential information about any Cayman Island entity for which they acted as London agents.

Kim decided to update Richard Black later and, instead, called Murray Jensen. He had quickly come to the view that more decisive action than he and Richard had discussed was now unavoidable. Kim wanted to put things in place, and then tell Richard, rather than debate the merits of what he had decided to do.

Chapter 37

Jackson and Ros checked into the flight quickly. There had only been two others in the business class check-in queue in front of them. Likewise, their priority pass saw them clear the security checks in no time at all. They headed to the Qantas Business Lounge.

The pair talked briefly about the meetings they had arranged for London. They were to see both of Jason's contacts in the afternoon on Monday, and Arthur Derwent on Tuesday. They knew what to expect in the Monday meetings, but the Tuesday one was by far the most important. If Jason was right, Arthur Derwent may well be the key to unlocking the burning question in each of their minds: Was the deal part of a criminal conspiracy to launder money?

'It's a long way to go in search of information to kill off the best deal I've ever worked on,' lamented Jackson, his deep blue eyes clouding over.

Ros' beautiful green eyes stared back at his. She put her hand over his. 'We both know why we have to do this. Let's just pray that it doesn't turn out to be an unacceptable risk for either of us.'

Jackson thought her words had a prophetic sound to them, but he dismissed the thought as he enjoyed the warmth from her hand.

They had something to eat and spent the next hour quietly reading the novels they had each brought with them. They boarded the A380 uneventfully, stowed their carry-on luggage in the ample space provided and settled into their very comfortable seats.

When the business class steward offered pre-take-off drinks, Jackson hesitated momentarily before accepting a vintage French champagne. It made him again think of his estranged wife. The two of them had a tradition of partaking in a French champagne before the departure of any long-haul flight.

His thoughts of Mary were interrupted by a very seductive Ros. 'Cheers, Tom. Here's to a great flight, and a successful series of meetings in London.'

'Cheers, and agreed.' Jackson clinked his glass against hers.

After take-off, Jackson saw that one of his all-time favourite movies, *Gladiator*, was on the classic movies list. He decided to watch it while he waited for the supper he'd selected to arrive. This would be his fourth meal today, but Jackson always travelled better if he ate regularly. He saw that Ros had chosen not to order supper, and was already curling up to sleep. She smiled warmly in his direction before snuggling in to her blanket and rolling over.

Chapter 38

Murray Jensen was pleased to receive another call from George Kim so soon after his operative Sarina's success yesterday. He had seen the reports of Ian Fox's unfortunate demise in a single-vehicle accident. The accident investigators had quickly concluded that excessive speed was involved, and that there were no suspicious circumstances. He was impressed at how well Sarina's skills had grown in such a short time, and with her obvious ability to improvise.

Kim had called Jensen on his secure line 'Well executed yesterday. Pun intended, of course.'

Jensen thought there was something sinister about Kim's muted chuckle that followed. Even though Murray was a seasoned operator, the sound sent a brief chill through him. He was well aware that George Kim was part of a very powerful crime syndicate and, while he was happy to have him as a client, he was fearful of one day falling short of the very high expectations that the man demanded.

'Our pleasure, of course.' Murray's response was professional, and no different from the response any other professional might provide to a satisfied client for a job well done. 'How can we further assist you?'

Kim explained the latest developments, and they discussed the alternative courses of action available.

'What about discouraging the contact Jackson and Green plan to see at Mathers Crompton on Tuesday?' offered Jensen.

'We have no way of knowing what Arthur Derwent may or may not be prepared to tell them.' George was more forceful now, clearly wishing to assert his authority as client. 'We have used Mathers Crompton as our Cayman agents for close to two decades, and there has never been any hint of a breach of confidence. I am almost certain that is not about to start now. They have always chosen their staff very carefully. Jackson and Green, on the other hand, are getting way too close for comfort.'

Kim told Jensen what he had in mind, and, as usual, left the detail to Murray.

Jensen knew where Tom Jackson and Ros Green were to stay in London and roughly when they would arrive at their hotel. Miles Fletcher had been able to glean this information from Jackson's private email account. Jackson had added information on the meetings to the detailed itinerary that Samantha Brown had prepared, and he had emailed it back to her. He always organised a comprehensive itinerary for every trip, in case someone needed to track him down in case of emergency. Well, this was an emergency, just not the sort he would be expecting.

Chapter 39

Murray Jensen had reflected on the call from George Kim overnight. Kim's call had been late Friday in London, early Saturday in Hong Kong. Jensen had decided to involve his most senior London operative and best asset, Charles Sanderson. Sanderson had been with Jensen for close to ten years, and Murray trusted him implicitly. He had never failed to deliver, even in the most difficult circumstances.

Like Jensen, Charles Sanderson was usually working in the office on a Saturday morning. It was their unofficial weekly briefing opportunity. 'Can you clear the decks for me, Charles,' Jensen commenced speaking as he entered his operative's adjacent office.

'Sure, guv. What's up?' Sanderson was a man of few words, as were many in the industry.

Jensen spent thirty minutes or so updating Charles on the roles they had been instructed to undertake by George Kim. Sanderson straightened in his seat slightly at the name. He too was well aware of the value of Kim and his syndicate as a client, and acutely aware of the need to always execute instructions from this client to the letter, without fail. The consequences of failure did not bear thinking about.

'The Rembrandt Hotel, you say?' queried Sanderson.

Jensen nodded.

'That's near the South Kensington Tube station.' He did not wait for Murray's reply. 'I suggest I shadow them to the station, where they'll surely go to head to their scheduled meetings on Monday, and see what opportunities present.'

Jensen agreed, subject to the need to ensure that he minimised as far as possible his exposure to the comprehensive CCTV network that the London authorities had installed almost everywhere since the 2005 bombings, and were always upgrading.

They both knew what the desired end result was, and also that events hardly ever unfolded as planned. Part of the secret of Murray Jensen's success, and of those who worked for him, was a very clear understanding of the need to allow events to develop organically, and to have the ability to quickly adapt and improvise. Sarina George's success the day before was a prime example of this.

Jensen had excellent detail and organisational skills, and was happiest when directing a hunt and kill operation somewhere in the world. It never ceased to amaze him how much people would pay to have some-one neutralised.

Chapter 40

Richard Black, CEO of Pacific Property, was a little unhappy to receive George Kim's call on Saturday afternoon. His concerns were twofold. Firstly, that Kim had not consulted him on such an important matter and, secondly, that any slip up may implicate Richard personally.

'I accept that you have the authority to make decisions of this magnitude, but I would have appreciated it if you had called me to discuss this before activating Murray Jensen.' Richard chose his words carefully. Kim was not one to be on the wrong side of.

'You're too close to aspects of this, Richard. Besides, a measure of separation should benefit you if anything does not go according to plan,' Kim replied. They both knew that Jensen had never failed to successfully complete a task, but there was always a first time.

Richard accepted this without further question. 'Okay. I agree, and will leave it to you and Murray Jensen to sort out the detail.'

He was glad that they had spent the money on providing secure lines for calls such as these.

Chapter 41

DAY 7 (Sunday)

The flight to Tokyo was a smooth one. Jackson and Ros were both gently awakened by the steward, who indicated that breakfast would shortly be served.

Jackson thought he had probably had around five hours of solid sleep. Ros had not stirred until now. She yawned and smiled brightly at Jackson before edging herself out of her seat and heading for the bathroom. He enjoyed watching how she stretched her limbs as she made her way forward. When she returned she looked amazing. *How can she look so alluring after a ten-hour flight?* They chatted briefly until breakfast arrived, each admitting to being a little excited about spending time together. That did not detract, however, from their apprehension about the next few days.

Before they knew it, they were on the ground in Tokyo and disembarking. *The Japanese are so organised and respectful,* Jackson thought to himself as they entered the Haneda Terminal and headed to the Qantas Business Lounge to have a shower and change of clothes. They only had a brief stopover, but it was certainly long enough to shower, change and stretch their legs a little.

Jackson and Ros headed to the shower area together, where they each surrendered their boarding passes for the next leg in exchange for a clean towel and a number for a particular shower recess. Ros looked at Tom as he invited her to go in front of him. She hesitated for only a moment before heading into the segregated female section. Jackson thought he saw her blushing, almost as if she was aware of his lustful thoughts. Not for the first time, his eyes wandered over her slim yet athletic physique, accentuated by the body-hugging outfit she was wearing.

'Up for a stroll?' invited Jackson when meeting up in the lounge afterwards.

'You know me,' grinned Ros. 'Always up for a little exercise. How much better does that feel after a shower, and some fresh underwear,' she continued, blushing slightly.

Jackson stood still briefly, imagining what could be. Ros visibly swallowed as she let out a sigh and touched his arm.

They collected their carry-on luggage from the locker area and headed off into the orderly throng of people milling about the terminal.

It wasn't long before they were boarding their flight for the next leg of their journey. At a little over twelve hours, this was slightly longer than the first leg. Thinking ahead to arrival time, around 1:00 p.m. London time, Jackson had decided to remain awake for most of the journey. That way, he reasoned, it would be easier to settle into local time on arrival. He knew he would be tired by the end of the day, but also knew from experience that he would sleep better and be more alert for the meetings over the next two days.

Chapter 42

Jackson was pleasantly surprised at how quickly they had cleared customs and immigration. This was notwithstanding the fact that London Heathrow was one of the busiest airports in the world, and that security was these days in a perpetual state of high alert.

The first thing they noticed as they emerged from the terminal was how bitterly cold it was. It was around 3 degrees, but the wind made it feel much cooler. Both Ros and Jackson had dressed for the change in season, but nothing could really prepare him for the initial shock of such a quantum shift in climate.

'While we were waiting in the immigration line I ordered an Uber for us,' Ros sounded more businesslike now. 'The driver will meet us in the pickup area of level 1 of the public short-stay carpark. It looks like he's only ten minutes away.'

Jackson was a big fan of the Uber ride-sharing service. How much more convenient was it to not have to give directions or fumble around for cash or a credit card at the end of the journey, at the same time as wanting to retrieve luggage and move on to whatever was next.

The Uber driver found them relatively easily. 'Good call. Thanks, Ros,' said Jackson as he buckled his seatbelt. 'The train from here is pretty good, but door-to-door is far more convenient.'

'No dramas,' replied Ros.

Jackson had noticed that, apart from a couple of power naps, Ros had also not had much sleep on the last flight. Yet she looked remarkably fresh and alert. *This will be a great opportunity to get to know each other better,* he thought.

The traffic was heavier than either of them had expected, but they were not in a hurry. In a little under an hour, they arrived at their destination, The Rembrandt Hotel, in South Kensington. Jackson had recalled on the way that he and Mary had stayed there in 2012 while they were in London for the Olympics.

'It's a beautiful old hotel with elegant but modern rooms, and with a great little bar area downstairs.' Jackson had said to Ros during the ride. 'Not that we'll have much time for sight-seeing, except perhaps for this afternoon, but the hotel is near the South Kensington Tube station, and only a few stops from the centre of Soho, which is always fun to visit.'

Ros had not stayed in Kensington before, and on entering the hotel, she seemed immediately impressed with Jackson's taste. The reception and bar areas were tastefully decorated and oozed style and comfort. A crackling fire place would have completed the picture, but these had been banned in many parts of London for some time. Some boroughs still permitted them, so long as they used an approved 'smokeless' fuel.

Somewhat to Jackson's relief, he and Ros were allocated rooms opposite each other on level 3.

Even though it was only mid-afternoon, they had to remind themselves that they had been in transit for more than twenty-four hours. They agreed to meet in the reception area in half an hour, allowing enough time to unpack, shower and change. Layers were the key to winter in London. Ros had expressed a keen interest in visiting the Carnaby Street precinct in Soho. They were both familiar with the area, which was usually bustling with shoppers and sightseers enjoying the wide variety of dining and shopping options.

Chapter 43

Mary Jackson awoke on the Sunday morning feeling a little anxious. While she had left Tom for good reason, that didn't mean she'd ceased caring for him. She had an uneasy feeling about his hands-on approach to the Pacific deal, particularly with the peripheral events that were unfolding around them.

Mary showered and dressed and decided on impulse to head out to what used to be her and her estranged husband's favourite coffee shop, the German Bakery in Taringa, for a coffee and croissant. The usual crowd at the bakery would hopefully serve to relieve the uneasy feeling she just couldn't seem to shake.

As she grabbed her keys and headed for her car in the garage, her mobile phone rang. Mary did not recognise the number that showed on the screen. 'Mary Jackson speaking.'

'Hi, Mary. We haven't met but my name is Jennifer Armitage. Sorry to bother you on a Sunday.'

Mary knew that Jennifer was one of the directors on the board of Pacific Property, and also that her partner, Ian Fox, had been tragically killed in a car accident two days ago. Mary's accounting firm was a competitor of Fox's firm, and they had often competed with each other for complex forensic accounting briefs. 'Tom has mentioned your name, Jennifer, and of course I knew Ian through work. I'm so sorry for your loss. Let me know if there is anything I can do for you.' Mary's tone was sympathetic.

'Can we meet, please? There's something I need to discuss with you.' Jennifer sounded very sad, but determined.

'Of course,' Mary replied quickly, feeling a little concerned, but had the good sense not to pursue the conversation any further by telephone. 'I was just heading to the German Bakery at Taringa for a coffee and croissant. Care to join me? We could get one of the outside tables, which are a little more private.'

'I know it. Good coffee. I live in Paddington, so could be there by nine. Does that suit?'

'Sounds fine. I'll get a table for us. See you then.' Mary wondered what Jennifer may have to say to her. Instinct told her it had to do with Jackson and the Pacific deal. Mary had seen the news item on Ian Fox on Friday, and she was aware of the connection to one of the directors at Pacific. She knew that the police traffic investigators had come to the conclusion that it was a single-vehicle accident involving excessive speed, and that there were no suspicious circumstances. They were still waiting on the results of more detailed toxicology tests but initial tests had been clear.

Chapter 44

'Sorry I'm a little late. Had trouble finding a park. I'm Jennifer Armitage.'

'Mary Jackson. Pleased to meet you' said Mary accepting Jennifer's outstretched hand. *Poor thing. She looks terrible,* Mary thought to herself as she gestured for Jennifer to take a seat.

Mary had selected an outside table farthest away from the others. The regular Sunday comings and goings of cars in the adjoining carpark would provide sufficient background noise to ensure that their discussion remained confidential.

'What would you like? I'll get it,' offered Mary.

'Large cappuccino, thanks. No food, please. I'm not hungry.' Mary saw that most of the queue had temporarily dissipated, so she jumped up and ordered two coffees, a croissant for her, and a sweet pastry for Jennifer. Even though Jennifer said she wasn't hungry, she looked like she could use something to eat, and Mary reasoned that she may change her mind when the pastry arrived.

Returning to the table, Mary again offered her condolences. Not without effort, Jennifer maintained her composure, and began. 'I know that Tom and Ros Green headed off to London together yesterday. I'm not exactly sure why, but I suspect it has something to do with the deal Tom has been working on for our company.' Mary was relieved that Jennifer was speaking in generalities, even though she was reasonably confident no one could hear their conversation.

Mary simply nodded and invited Jennifer to continue.

Jennifer looked around. The table next door was now vacant. 'I don't think Ian's death on Friday was an accident.' She was struggling to hold back tears now.

Mary was surprised. 'I've seen most of the news feeds on the tragic accident, and the police have concluded that it was just that. What makes you think otherwise?'

'I know it looks like it, but I don't believe it. Ian was a brilliant driver. His Porsche was almost new, and only recently serviced. Weather conditions on Friday were fine. He would never take any unnecessary risks. I've been in the car with him plenty of times, including on that very stretch of road. Sure, he loved speed but he was a very safe driver. A conservative one. He was a forensic accountant, whose life was dictated by logic.'

'Maybe it was just a very unfortunate coincidence.' Mary didn't believe what she'd just said, and, from the look on her face, neither did Jennifer.

'Ian had initiated some investigations into aspects of the deal, to try and help me out, before heading off on his fateful car trip.' Jennifer continued before Mary could say anything. 'In my naivety I have become involved in something I shouldn't have. Ian was just trying to help. I met yesterday with Ian's good friend and colleague, Ray Kean, and Ray is pursuing what Ian started. We know it may be dangerous, but we agreed we owe it to Ian. I know that you and Tom are not together any more but thought that, since he is away, I needed to talk to you to see if you could help. I hope you don't mind.'

Mary immediately knew that she should help. Obviously, the less people involved in this the better, but she was worried about Tom and realised that this may help him. 'Of course. What can I do?' she said, almost without hesitation.

Jennifer explained that she wanted Mary to discreetly let Jackson know that Ian's investigations were under way, and to set up a meeting with Tom when he got back to Brisbane on Thursday. Mary agreed. She could see no harm in that.

Their coffee and food had arrived. Jennifer gratefully accepted the food, nodding appreciatively to Mary as she began to devour the sweet pastry as though she hadn't eaten for at least twenty-four hours. She hadn't. They engaged in light conversation until they'd finished their coffees and parted company as new friends.

Chapter 45

On the way home, Mary decided to call Max Grenfell. 'Hi Max, it's Mary Jackson. Sorry for the interruption on a Sunday, but I wouldn't mind a quick chat with you if you have time?'

'Mary, sure. What's up?' Max usually only caught up with Mary a few times a year at work-related events, but he had always enjoyed her company. He hadn't seen her since she'd left Tom twelve months prior.

'I'm not far from your place. Would you mind if I dropped in for a brief chat?'

Max thought she sounded a little mysterious, but understood that it must be something she did not wish to discuss on the phone. 'No problem. Nellie and the kids are out, and I was not far away from heading out to join them.'

'Thanks, Max. Be there in ten.'

Mary parked in the driveway then was greeted by Max with a hug and peck on the cheek. 'I've set up a jug of iced water with lime on the back deck. Come through. Would you like a tea or coffee?'

'Water's fine, thanks Max. Sorry again to barge in on a Sunday, but this is important.'

'I gathered as much. Fire away. I'm all ears.'

'Has Tom kept you in the loop with what's been happening on his big deal with Pacific Property?'

'Yes,' responded Max. 'We usually chat on a daily basis about most things. It helps to be able to bounce things off someone with a similar moral compass. I am up to speed with what's going on and know Tom is in London with Ros Green to undertake some critical face-to-face meetings.'

Mary had expected that would be the case. 'I've just had coffee with Jennifer Armitage.'

Max sat up a little straighter in his chair. 'Do you know Jennifer?' he asked.

'Not before her call this morning, but of course I knew Ian Fox as I often fiercely competed with him for work.' Mary proceeded to tell Max what Jennifer had said to her this morning, including her suspicions that Ian's death may not have been an accident.

'Tom and I came to a similar conclusion when we discussed this on Friday.' The hair on Max's neck was standing up now. 'Isn't it time the authorities were involved?'

'I've thought about that too, and it's too soon. There are a lot of suspicious things happening, but more evidence is needed. I'm sure that's why Tom has become directly involved.' Mary pressed her lips together.

They both agreed that any involvement of the authorities would have to wait until Jackson and Ros had returned from London. To do otherwise may place their wellbeing at risk.

'I'll set up the meeting between Jennifer and Tom on Thursday afternoon. I'm pretty sure he's back that morning. I suggest you do not speak to anyone, including Tom, about Jennifer's visit today.'

'Thanks, Max. You're a good friend to Tom.' Mary got up to leave.

Max showed her to the door. 'Tom and I look out for each other. It helps to stay sane in the crazy environment we operate in.'

'I know. Thanks again.' Mary hopped in her car and drove off, knowing that she had done the right thing by passing Jennifer's information about the separate investigation on to Max.

As she drove away from Max's house, Mary was preoccupied with the events of the morning, and she failed to notice Sarina Georges' silver AMG Mercedes parked in an adjacent street.

Chapter 46

Buoyed by her success on Friday, Sarina had decided to keep an eye on Jackson's estranged wife's movements over the next couple of days. She knew Tom still kept in contact with her, and her professional contacts could be a threat if Jackson had confided any of his concerns with her. Murray Jensen had sent Sarina a secure message late on Friday, congratulating her on a job well done. He had informed her that Tom Jackson would be in London from Saturday until Thursday. She was to stand down and await further instructions.

She was reflecting on the events of the morning and wondering if it was worthy of a further report to Jensen. All she really knew was that Mary had met separately with Jennifer Armitage and Max Grenfell. They could be just friends catching up on a Sunday. Sarina had noticed that Mary and Jennifer had shaken hands, rather than embraced, so they weren't good friends. *So what?* she thought to herself. *Mary was better friends with Max, given the greeting he gave her, but that should not be surprising.*

Sarina decided not to call Jensen. It was after midnight on Saturday in London, and there was nothing specific she could tell him. Besides, he had asked her to stand down for now.

Chapter 47

The temperature had not changed at all since their arrival in London. It felt much colder than three degrees as Jackson and Ros left The Rembrandt Hotel, headed for the Tube station and Soho. Like Jackson, Ros had dressed in multiple layers so they could be progressively removed if they went indoors. Both were happy to stretch their legs and had decided to add a couple of extra blocks to their walk to the South Kensington Tube station.

Ros is good company, Jackson thought as they emerged from the Piccadilly Circus Tube station twenty minutes later. She had an engaging smile and laugh. It was nice for them to relax a little before the important meetings that lay ahead of them.

They wandered around Carnaby Street and surrounding areas, taking in the sights and sounds, and occasionally browsing through some of the more interesting gift shops.

'I'm really enjoying our time together.' Ros leaned closer to Tom, tilting her head up.

I could kiss her right now, although I probably shouldn't in public. But his primal urges took over, and he kissed her tenderly on the lips. They drew apart and held each other's gaze briefly before walking on through the ever-increasing throng of people.

The crowds were starting to arrive at the restaurants for their evening meal. 'Can you believe it's six o'clock already?' Jackson was surprised.

Ros grinned, linking her arm with his. 'Let's go back. Do you recall what the food is like at the hotel?'

'It's a few years since I stayed here, but I remember the food in the bar area was quite tasty.' Jackson shivered as they headed for the Tube station, walking in the opposite direction to the crowds. 'Why don't we go to the bar for a couple of drinks and a light meal? I can't recall how many meals I've eaten since we left Brisbane, but I'm certain that it's a few more than I should have.'

They both wore a contented smile as they clung to each other, having dropped the pretence of not being together. After all, it was cold and dark. The sun had set over an hour ago. London was a big place, and they were not expecting to see anyone they knew.

Chapter 48

Even though it was relatively early, it was Sunday, and the hotel bar was almost filled to capacity. They managed to find a small booth in a warm corner. That gave them a little space to place their jackets and gloves. Jackson threw his jacket on the same side of the booth as Ros' and slid into her side of the booth. 'This way we can both people watch while we warm each other with our body heat,' he said by way of explanation.

Ros didn't seem to mind at all. She smiled at him, her sparkling green eyes catching and holding his own deep blue ones as he gazed at her.

'I'll get us a drink. Do you have anything in mind?' Jackson could barely tear his gaze away from hers. The temptation of being around her, so far from home, was starting to get the better of him. God, she was beautiful. Not overtly, but with her platinum blond hair, creamy complexion, soft curves and penetrating green eyes, she exerted a sensual charisma that he'd always found attractive.

'I did rather enjoy that French champagne on the flight,' said Ros. Her voice was seductively husky, and her cheeks flushed red from the cold air. He knew he wasn't going to get away from this easily. And he wasn't sure he wanted to. He and Mary had been separated for over a year now, and as much as he missed her, his desire for Ros was growing by the minute.

'French champagne it is then. I'll get us each a glass.' Jackson was already on his way to the bar.

He returned with a bottle of vintage Veuve Clicquot. 'What?' he said when she stared at the bottle. 'They didn't sell the vintage Veuve by the glass. We don't have to drink it all.' Although the way his body was on fire, he just might need to.

'No complaints from me,' said Ros as Jackson poured her a generous glass.

Ros had studied the bar food menu while Jackson was getting the champagne. When the food waiter appeared, Ros ordered a selection of food to complement the champagne, without consulting Tom.

'Great choices. Exactly what I felt like,' Jackson agreed.

They chatted away about nothing in particular until the food arrived. Neither had realised just how hungry they were. Long distance travel and cold weather did that to you. Ros had chosen four different tapas-style dishes from the menu, and the quality and flavour of each was excellent.

After the plates were cleared away, Jackson poured the last of the bottle into their champagne flutes. They sat silently, side by side, watching the now-thinning crowd in the bar. The electricity between them was crackling as they leaned closer to one another.

'It's getting late.' Jackson interrupted their thoughts. 'I know it's only around 8:30 p.m. but we've come a long way and have a couple of big days ahead of us.'

Ros nodded her agreement, her eyes never leaving his.

After they had gathered their warm gear, Ros slid her arm inside Jackson's again, and they headed to the lift. Tom was happy to leave her arm where it was, and wondered silently at what lay ahead.

When they arrived at their rooms on either side of the hallway, Ros asked, "Nightcap? I noticed a small bottle of Veuve in the bar fridge. Not vintage, of course.' She winked.

'Why not.' Tom could feel his heart pounding.

Ros showed Jackson into her room, which was warmer than the bar area downstairs. She slowly peeled off another layer, revealing her slim and very fit curves, then moved in closer and embraced him. There was no resistance from Jackson as their lips met in a passionate kiss. He could feel her pressing against him and could hear her hot breath panting gently in his ear.

What am I doing? Jackson suddenly thought to himself as he moved away from her a little. 'I'm sorry, Ros,' he said apologetically.

'It's okay, and I'm not,' said Ros, removing her top to display a wonderful set of perfectly shaped breasts with large and erect pink nipples.

Jackson's eyes drank in her curvaceous body, which was naked from the waist up. Giving in to his temptations, Tom embraced her as they hungrily undressed each other. His skin was tingling with pleasure as her expert hands gently caressed his manhood. He heard an audible intake of breath as she responded to his touch. He shivered from pleasure and desire as he entered her. Ros moaned loudly. Both cried out at the same time as they reached their climax together. Afterwards, they lay in each other's arms for some time before Jackson reluctantly decided he should return to his room and get some sleep before the big day ahead.

Chapter 49

Not long after returning to his room, Jackson's mobile phone rang. It was Mary calling on Skype. Tom collected his thoughts. He wasn't expecting to hear from Mary while in London. It was close to 10:30 pm in London, so around 7:30 a.m. in Brisbane on Monday morning.

With a sharp pang of remorse, he answered the call. 'Mary, I wasn't expecting to hear from you. Is everything okay?'

'I met with Max Grenfell yesterday morning.' Mary got straight to the point without exchanging any pleasantries. 'I had to speak to him about something that happened earlier in the morning.'

'Are you alright?' A shiver went through Jackson.

'Yes, fine. It's not really something I can elaborate on via Skype. Suffice to say that Max is setting up a meeting for you on Thursday afternoon.' Mary sounded concerned, and maybe a little detached, Jackson thought, or was that just his guilty imagination?

'I understand. Thanks, Mary,' replied Jackson, sounding calmer than he felt, and wondering to himself what the meeting with Max might be about.

'I'll leave you to it then. I hope it all goes well for you in London.' Mary ended the call.

Jackson knew that neither of them trusted the privacy of international call technology. He was relieved that she didn't engage him in any discussion on events so far.

Chapter 50

DAY 8 (Monday)

Jackson slept in a little, which was easier to do when the sun didn't rise until around 8:00 a.m. Their first meeting was not until early afternoon with Jason Jones' key contacts, so a little extra rest was not detrimental to their schedule. As he left his room and headed for the breakfast area on the ground floor, Jackson noticed that Ros had a 'Please make up my room' sign on her door. He hoped she was still at breakfast. He had no regrets about what had taken place the night before, and he wanted to ensure she was also comfortable. He didn't want there to be any awkwardness between them.

It was towards the end of the breakfast session, and there weren't many people still in the dining room. To his relief, Jackson saw that one of them was Ros. She waved to him as he headed towards her table.

'Morning, Tom.'

She sounded bright and cheery, Jackson thought, but then she always did.

'Morning, Ros. Sleep well?' Tom wasn't sure whether to pretend nothing had happened, or if he should talk openly about it. He decided to let Ros take the lead on this.

'Thank you for last night. I haven't felt that level of joy and satisfaction in such a long time.' Ros had a cheeky grin on her face as she winked at him.

'My absolute pleasure. The feeling is mutual.' Tom didn't know why he needed to feel relieved, but he did. *Maybe there is something real between us we can pursue.* But he felt it was too early to share his innermost feelings. He could see from her distant gaze that she might be having similar thoughts.

'Our meetings are at 12:30 p.m. and 2:30 p.m.,' Jackson reminded them both, in an endeavour to redirect the conversation. It worked. Ros shook her head almost imperceptibly, as if to shake off the euphoric feeling.

Resuming her usual professional demeanour, Ros responded, 'I've been looking at the logistics of getting around. We can catch the Tube at South Kensington just around the corner. Both meetings are within walking distance of the Blackfriars Tube station, which is only seven stops away on the Circle Line.'

Jackson had already researched this before he'd left Australia, but he was happy to let Ros continue.

'Why don't we head off straight after breakfast? That should give us enough time to get off at somewhere like Westminster and have a bit of a look around. I always get a rush when I visit historical places like Westminster Abbey. It's been a while since I've been there, and it will be special to share that experience with you.' Ros reverted to the dreamy look she had earlier.

'Sounds fine to me,' said Jackson, involuntarily mimicking her expression.

Chapter 51

When he returned to the reception area at the appointed time, Jackson saw that Ros was shrugging into her coat, having already donned her scarf, gloves and warm hat. Tom quickly joined her in this ritual.

'Ready?' Ros beamed, hooking her arm though this.

'Ready as I'll ever be. Let's go.'

Tom had checked his Weather Channel App, so was expecting it to feel like minus-one degree outside. He was still not fully prepared for the cold, and his breath was taken away as they left the hotel and headed for the Tube station.

Ros kept her head down in an effort to minimise the amount of skin that was exposed to the cold. Jackson could see from her expression how happy she was. She smiled tenderly at him when she noticed he was looking.

He was always excited to travel on the London Underground and never ceased to marvel at the incredible foresight shown by the British forefathers. Imagine the number of naysayers when it was suggested in the mid-nineteenth century that an underground train line be built in London.

As they arrived at the station, Jackson saw that it was packed with commuters. He remembered that Londoners started work later in winter than they did in summer.

'Don't get crowds like this in Brisbane,' Jackson had to shout over the noise of the throng and the train departing in the opposite direction.

'Won't have to wait long,' Ros shouted back. 'Even if we don't get on the next train, there'll be another along a couple of minutes after.'

Ros was right. They didn't make it onto the next train, but a large mass of humanity did. They edged closer to the line on the edge of the platform, and were at the front of the pack to board the next train that was due in two minutes.

Jackson was not ready for what happened next. He heard the train approaching and turned in its direction. Ros was standing right next to him. Then he heard a bloodcurdling scream, and his head snapped back to Ros to see what had happened. She was no longer next to him.

'Oh my fucking God. She jumped,' said someone who was standing next to the spot where Ros should have been.

'Why do they have to choose a Monday morning to do that?' complained another commuter standing behind Jackson.

Tom wasn't sure what he was going on about. He had heard that the Circle Line was often stopped on a Monday morning to deal with 'service difficulties'. He knew this to be a euphemism for the need to scrape someone off the track who had decided it was all too much for them.

Where the hell was Ros? Jackson was tall and even though he was sure Ros wouldn't have moved away from their ready boarding position, he scanned the nearby crowd to see if he could see her. She was nowhere to be seen.

Then it suddenly dawned on him. He turned to the woman he thought he'd heard scream. 'What happened!' he yelled at her.

'That woman standing next to you launched herself onto the track in front of the oncoming train!'

What was she saying? Was Ros gone? How could that have happened? One moment she was there, and the next she was gone.

Jackson was searching the crowd for some clue as to what might have happened. 'Are you sure she wasn't pushed?' He felt like he was about to be physically ill.

'Sorry, guv. She jumped,' said the man who had complained moments ago. 'Sadly, it happens a lot on the Circle Line, especially on a Monday morning.'

'What are you talking about!' Jackson roared. 'She wasn't suicidal. She must have been pushed!' He again scanned the faces of the nearby crowd. Each of them was averting their eyes from his and sadly shaking their heads. They could see that he was distressed and did not want to look him in the eye any longer than was necessary.

Things ground to a halt very quickly, and the police were on the scene almost immediately. It was as if they had a practiced procedure to deal with this. The crowd quickly dispersed to seek alternative means of transport. The Circle Line would be shut down for a couple of hours while the tracks were cleaned and an investigation was carried out.

Chapter 52

Charles Sanderson had furtively followed Tom Jackson and Ros Green to Soho the day before. He preferred to spend as much time as possible watching his quarry. It allowed him to observe behavioural patterns that often proved useful to the implementation of his plan.

Sanderson had been a professional soldier and sniper before he'd met Murray Jensen at a gym almost ten years ago and had been persuaded to join his growing business. Charles was built like an ox and had the strength of one. At forty-one, he had the physique of a much younger man. He had shaved his head, had arms and legs like a body builder, and the three large folds of skin at the base of his skull were the only suggestion that he did have a neck. Sanderson wore a permanent scowl on his face and his crooked mouth made it look like he was always on the verge of a snarl.

He was certain that Ros was infatuated with Jackson, but he was unable to determine if the feeling was mutual. He detected mixed messages from Jackson, but their walk back to the hotel after leaving the Tube station left him in no doubt about how Ros felt about the handsome lawyer.

In order to avoid detection, Sanderson had decided not to continue his surveillance of the pair after they'd returned to their hotel.

He had returned early in the morning to take up the vantage point he'd identified the day before. From there he could see both the hotel entrance and the road Jackson and Ros would need to take to get to the South Kensington Tube station.

He was rewarded for his diligence and patience when they left the hotel together not long after 10:00 a.m. and headed for the Tube station. *Very promising*, Charles had thought to himself. *At this hour in winter, the Tube station will still be crawling with commuters.* He'd quickly headed to the station to ensure he arrived first.

The hitman had been able to utilise his considerable skills to place himself in the crowd adjacent to Jackson and Ros. Charles was tall but as luck would have it, he was surrounded by a number of tall commuters, who were also still wearing hats and scarves. He had taken note of where the CCTV cameras were and felt he had positioned himself well, should an opportunity present itself. It did. As the train they were about to catch began to arrive, most turned in the direction of the train. As Ros turned, she was momentarily off balance. The slight nudge from him exaggerated her imbalance, and made it look as if she had flung herself in front of the train just as the front carriage was about to pass their position.

Sanderson calmly left with the rest of the commuters, keen to be gone by the time the authorities arrived to begin their investigation. He noticed that the nearby woman who'd screamed loudly had remained to comfort Jackson.

Chapter 53

Transport security and police were on the scene almost immediately. Experience had taught them that the London commuters would want to get where they needed to be, and so would disperse quickly.

Tom was still staring at the train. Ros was under there somewhere. He couldn't believe it. Surely this was a mistake. It was someone else and Ros would appear shortly with her smiling face, asking what happened.

'Are you alright?' asked the woman who had remained behind to comfort him. She also thought it would be useful for the police to hear her version of events. 'Did you know her?'

Jackson was still in shock. Slowly the awful truth began to dawn on him. He realised that, apart from the woman standing next to him, and a few others who were mostly in uniform, the mass of humanity that had been present only a matter of minutes ago was now almost gone.

'Did you know her?' It was a man's voice this time. Jackson saw that he was being addressed by a police officer, and nodded.

The woman next to him identified herself and offered to assist with a statement. 'I saw the whole unfortunate event. That poor woman jumped.'

Tom still couldn't believe what he was hearing. 'But there is no reason for her to have done that,' he mumbled, almost to himself. He was devastated, especially after the new bond he felt they had begun to forge together. He had detected that she too was happy about what they'd shared and what might lay ahead, but that had all been snuffed out in the blink of an eye. *Jumped?* It didn't make any sense.

Chapter 54

The police were very efficient. Tom and the witness were taken to a nearby command centre and interviewed.

'Are you sure there is nothing you're aware of that may have led her to take her own life?' the policemen asked Jackson.

He'd collected his thoughts on the way to the command centre and had resolved not to tell the police too much about why he and Ros were in London. He had thought about telling them about the events of the night before, but then decided against it. Ros was an intelligent and headstrong woman. Surely she would not commit suicide out of any misguided sense of morality. Would she?

'Nothing at all, sorry,' said Jackson, more in control now. 'As I've mentioned, we are – were, sorry – in London on business together and were heading to one of our scheduled meetings in the city.'

'Very well, sir. Thank you for your cooperation. We have your details and will most likely wish to interview you again after we've reviewed all the CCTV footage available.'

Jackson did not know that a lightning quick review of the CCTV footage, from all angles, had already been undertaken by trained operatives. He and the female witness were only being allowed to leave because that review had not in any way implicated either of them in the incident. A more comprehensive review was already underway.

Chapter 55

Charles Sanderson did not take pleasure in killing. He was a professional not a psychopath. He was very good at his job, however, and took pride in his work.

He called Murray Jensen, adopting their agreed code. 'Busy morning, guv. Some poor woman jumped onto the Circle Line tracks at South Kensington. I managed to switch to the Piccadilly Line without suffering too much delay. I'll be in the office soon.'

Jensen remained silent and terminated the call, grinning to himself. They say one of the secrets to success is to surround yourself with good people. He reflected on just how fortunate he'd been at achieving just that. It was no accident, of course. He was passionate about what he did and very careful about selecting and training the people who worked for him.

Murray looked at his watch and decided to call George Kim immediately with the good news. It would be around 7:00 p.m. Monday evening in Hong Kong. He knew their line was secure.

When Kim answered, Murray said, 'I've just heard. Ros Green has just had a nasty accident. It seems she threw herself in front of a train.'

'Very efficient, as usual.' George Kim was not usually complimentary but was genuinely happy with the results Jensen had achieved for him. 'I take it there were no issues?'

'None whatsoever.' Murray sounded confident, even though he had not yet had a chance to discuss with Charles any potential risks with witnesses and CCTV footage.

'Let's see what Jackson does now. He should get the message loud and—' George Kim said this almost to himself and ended the call as he was finishing his sentence.

*

First Ian Fox and now poor Ros, Jackson thought to himself as he headed back to the hotel. He needed some time to think about this. Were they really both accidents or were there sinister forces at play here? As Tom did not believe in coincidences at all, and particularly not coincidences of this magnitude, he had to assume the latter.

He needed to speak to Jason Jones, he decided. It would still be relatively early on Monday evening in Brisbane.

Chapter 56

Jason Jones answered his mobile phone on the first ring. 'Hey Jason, that was quick. Have you got your mobile glued to your hand?' Jackson began, trying unsuccessfully to lighten his own mood.

'You okay, mate? Wasn't expecting to hear from you so soon,' Jason replied

'Ros Green is dead.'

'What the fuck! How, and are you okay?'

'Are calls to your phone digitally encrypted?' Jackson thought they would be, but wanted to be sure.

'Sure are, mate. Fire away.'

Jackson described in detail the events of the morning while Jason listened intently. 'It all happened so fast. One moment she was standing next to me, and the next she was under the train. Witnesses say she jumped, and the police are checking the CCTV footage. I'm having a lot of difficulty coming to terms with the fact that she's gone.'

Careful, Tom. There's no point in letting anyone think that there was some kind of romantic connection between us, and particularly not someone with such highly trained instincts as Jason Jones.

'The cops will have already checked the CCTV. I know how they work. They wouldn't have let you go so quickly if they hadn't done that. I'm sure you're not a suspect or anything, but that mob have learnt the hard way. They are very thorough. Fuck Tom, what are you planning to do now?'

'I was hoping you'd have a view on that. My current thinking is that I'll skip the meetings with your two contacts today and lay low. That will also leave me free to speak to the police again if they require me to.'

'Good plan. I'll fix that.' Jason cut in. 'Nothing new there anyway.'

'I'm still thinking of seeing Arthur Derwent at Mathers Crompton tomorrow afternoon. He's my best chance of uncovering something. I feel I owe it to Ros.'

'Agreed,' Jason said quickly. 'You will need to be extra careful from here, Tom. I know you can handle yourself, but give that fucking public transport a miss, mate. Too dangerous. I'll arrange a driver I know and trust. He's a Tae Kwon Do master and a bloody handy bodyguard. Russell's his name. Big bastard. I'll get him to pick you up from your hotel an hour before your meeting. He'll wait and take you to the airport after your meeting and stay with you until you board your flight at midnight. There'll be a fair amount of waiting around, but you'll be safe.'

'Thanks, Jason. I knew you'd have a better idea than me about what to do.' He felt a moderate amount of relief, but was still distraught about Ros. What a special day he had shared with her. Her last! He would never know now how far their new relationship may have progressed.

Chapter 57

The police did make contact again with Tom in the afternoon. They advised they had completed their investigation, and had made contact with Ros's next of kin to make arrangements for her body. The coroner would carry out toxicology tests first, but that was not expected to take long.

Very efficient, Jackson thought. 'Was there anything unusual on the CCTV?' he asked, knowing what the likely response would be.

'Nothing at all, sir. You are free to leave London on your scheduled flight tomorrow. Safe travels.'

Jackson was a little shocked at how professionally detached the constable had been. He guessed that was an essential attribute for an accident investigator in a city of over nine million people.

In an effort to try and take his mind off things, Tom read through his emails. He saw with some satisfaction that his team was progressing well with the final stages of document negotiation for the Pacific deal, although he seriously doubted the deal would proceed.

Jackson's thoughts turned to Ros again. *Would she really do that to herself?* He doubted it very much, especially not after last night. He wondered if there was anyone else he should call, and decided that, for now, there wasn't. There would be plenty of time when he arrived back in Brisbane to speak to people like Richard Black who, presently, he did not trust at all.

Jackson closed his laptop and reached for the Ken Follett novel he had brought with him. He realised that it was mid-afternoon, and he hadn't yet eaten lunch. He ordered room service even though he wasn't very hungry, but thought he should eat something substantial that would also serve as an early dinner. He didn't even want to go downstairs in the hotel for a meal.

The thought occurred to him to call hotel reception and tell them about Ros.

'The police have already been in contact with us, sir. We are liaising with the next of kin through them. We are very saddened by her passing.'

Very efficient, and almost mechanical, Jackson thought again.

Chapter 58

DAY 9 (Tuesday)

Jackson had slept fitfully the night before. Every time he'd awoken, he'd had to remind himself that the nightmare was real. He'd managed to fall into a deep sleep early in the morning and didn't wake until close to 9:00 a.m. There was still time to make breakfast downstairs.

He was able to arrange a late checkout at 1:30 p.m., when Russell was supposed to pick him up. His meeting with Arthur Derwent was at 2:30 p.m.

Russell arrived out the front of the hotel at 1:25 p.m. in a black Chrysler 300C. Jackson had always thought of the 300C as a muscle car. As Russell unfolded himself from the vehicle, Tom could see that Jason was right. Russell was huge. With a broad smile he held out a massive hand to greet Jackson, as if he were a long-lost friend.

'Great to see you again,' boomed Russell, gripping Jackson with a very firm handshake. Jason must have sent Russell a photo, thought Tom.

'Likewise,' replied Jackson, glad to have his hand returned to him in one piece.

Russell stooped to collect Jackson's luggage and stowed it in the boot without the slightest amount of effort.

To maintain the guise, Jackson hopped in the front seat as Russell folded himself back in to the driver's seat. As they drove off, the big man said, 'Jason has asked me to look after you until your flight leaves at midnight tonight. It'll be my pleasure, sir.'

'I appreciate it,' Jackson thanked him. 'We're headed for the Mathers Crompton office for a 2:30 p.m. meeting.'

'Already in the sat nav, sir. It's not that far but the sat nav will take us the fastest route available. It's always peak hour in London. It can take up to an hour sometimes to get through the traffic.'

Jackson's feelings were mixed. He felt very uncomfortable that he needed protection, but at the same time incredibly relieved that he had it. He was exhausted but knew he had to speak with Arthur Derwent.

Chapter 59

Jackson arrived in the reception of Mathers Crompton fifteen minutes early. He always felt more comfortable being a little early. It gave him an opportunity to mentally rehearse some of the questions he planned to ask.

'I'm here to meet with Arthur Derwent at 2:30 p.m. I'm a little early. My name's Tom Jackson.'

The receptionist looked up at him, smiling. 'I'm sorry, sir, but Arthur is not in today. He called in sick first thing. There are some nasty bugs going around at the moment. Standard fare for London in winter, I'm afraid.'

'No one called me to tell me he was not in.' Jackson was angry. 'I'm heading back to Australia this evening, and I must speak with Arthur today. Can you please give me his mobile number.'

'Sorry, sir. It's against our privacy policy to do that. Lawyers are of course free to provide you with their mobile numbers, but if he hasn't done so, I can't assist.'

It wasn't her fault, and he didn't want to make any kind of scene. What would that achieve? He quickly decided to leave and call Jason Jones from Russell's car to see if he had Arthur's mobile number.

Russell was waiting beside his car, and, if he was surprised at Jackson's early return, he didn't show it.

'Jason, sorry to call you so late.' Tom explained to Jones what had happened and asked if he had Arthur Derwent's mobile.

'No worries about the late call, mate. I do have his mobile number and will log on to my computer and grab it. I wonder if the prick's been told not to meet with you. Can you stay on the line while I call him on my second line?'

While he waited, Jackson wondered if Jason was right. Had Arthur Derwent been warned off meeting with him?

Jason interrupted his thoughts. 'I reckon he's been shut down, mate. He has a fucking voice message saying he's ill, can't take the call, and doesn't know when he'll be feeling well enough to return the call. This is the same shit that happened to me while I was investigating last week. I think you should get Russell to take you to the airport early. He can park in the special permit area and stay with you in the business class lounge until you leave.'

Jackson thought of protesting, out of sheer frustration. But what good would that do? 'Thanks, Jason. I appreciate everything you've done so far. I know you're right, but I thought I could achieve something by coming to London. All I've managed to do is get Ros killed.' He was starting to get upset. This was out of character for him, but he was still reeling from yesterday's events and hadn't had much sleep.

'Not your fault. Don't blame yourself. Just get home in one piece and we can regroup and see where we go from here.'

Chapter 60

DAY 10 (Wednesday)

The first part of the trip back to Brisbane was a blur for Jackson. He vaguely recalled farewelling Russell in the business class lounge at Heathrow, after a long but relatively silent afternoon and evening together. It had been good to feel safe, after all that had happened. The empty seat beside him on the plane was, however, a constant reminder that Ros was gone.

It was not until he showered and changed in Tokyo that he was able to refocus. He had managed to sleep most of the way from London to Tokyo, and was now feeling refreshed and beginning to collect his thoughts.

One step at a time, Tom reminded himself once again of Mary Jackson's simple but very practical advice. He had called Mary from the airport in London to let her know that Ros had been killed and to make sure that she was safe. Mary had expressed shock at what had happened to Ros and had implored Tom not to take any more unnecessary risks.

Jackson planned to head home, change and then head into the office for his meeting with Max Grenfell.

Chapter 61

He emerged from the immigration and customs area at Brisbane International Airport about half an hour after the plane landed. Jackson had travelled a long way for nothing, and Ros was dead. He was relieved to be home, and to his surprise Mary was there to greet him at the arrival gate. She had a look of concern on her face.

They hugged briefly like old friends, but not as a husband and wife would. *Almost like old times,* Tom thought, at least until Mary said she had made the trip to meet him to make sure he was okay and to elaborate more on the meeting Max had arranged.

'I'm glad you're back safely, Tom,' Mary began as they drove out of the short-stay car park. They were both silent for a few minutes. Mary wasn't sure if Tom wanted to talk about Ros, so thought she would leave that to him to raise. 'How did the meeting on Tuesday afternoon go?'

'It didn't,' said Jackson despondently.

Mary glanced sideways at Tom, who continued, 'Arthur Derwent was ill, not in the office and completely uncontactable. Just another one of many coincidences. But I can't believe Ros was standing next to me one minute and gone the next.'

'God, that's terrible. Did the police get back to you?'

'Yes. Predictably they said that a comprehensive review of the CCTV footage did not show anything suspicious. They concluded that Ros killed herself. I know that's bullshit, but I have no way of proving it.' To change the subject Jackson asked, 'What's this about a meeting with Max this afternoon?'

'Actually, Max has set up a meeting with Jennifer Armitage.' Mary proceeded to tell Jackson about her meeting with Jennifer on Sunday morning, and her subsequent meeting with Max.

'I'm sorry you have become so deeply involved in this, whatever this is,' was all Jackson could think of to say.

Chapter 62

Max Grenfell had scheduled the meeting for 3:00 p.m. in one of the meeting rooms at Ridgeway Mason. Jackson was not sure that was such a good idea, with scoundrels like Roger Everingham and Miles Fletcher snooping around, but he trusted Max's judgement.

Tom arrived in the office a little before 2:30 p.m. and headed straight to Max's office. Max was waiting for him. He knew Tom would prefer to brainstorm with him ahead of the meeting with Jennifer Armitage so had cleared his schedule.

'How are you holding up, Tom? We've all heard the terrible details of Ros' demise. I'm really sorry, mate.' Max was genuinely sympathetic and concerned for Jackson's wellbeing.

Tom was relieved to be back home, and to have a good friend and colleague such as Max to help him get through this. He had felt so isolated in London. 'Thanks, Max. Not much anyone could have done. I'm certain it was no accident, but I believe the police investigated thoroughly and concluded that it was suicide. I'm not sure how they did it, but she was standing right next to me. There is absolutely no way someone like Ros would do that to herself.' *Focus, Tom,* he reminded himself. *If for no other reason than you owe it to Ros.*

For now, he had decided not to tell anyone about their passionate encounter on Sunday evening. There was nothing to be gained by sharing that information.

'Any leads from your London meetings?' Max enquired.

'Believe it or not, I actually didn't attend any meetings.' Jackson told Max he had skipped the meetings with Jason Jones' contacts on Monday, and that his Tuesday meeting at Mathers Crompton had effectively been blocked. 'It was an incredibly frustrating exercise, and one which, in hindsight, I wish I'd never embarked upon.'

'Don't be too hard on yourself. Has Mary filled you in on the details of her meeting with Jennifer Armitage?' Jackson nodded, and Max continued. 'Let's hope she can shed some more light on this. Even if she isn't able to, you should probably go to the authorities anyway.'

'With what?' Jackson felt the anger well up inside him, but managed to keep it in check. It wasn't Max's fault. He was just trying to help. 'My car was clipped, but I didn't get any identifying information. Mary may have been followed by the same person, but there is no way to be sure. Ian Fox was killed in a tragic single-vehicle accident, with no suspicious circumstances, according to the police. Ros, again according to the police, decided to throw herself in front of a train in London. Last, but by no means least, Arthur Derwent was ill and uncontactable. Sure, Jason Jones has uncovered rumours of the gambling debt owed by James Yeo, and has made a tenuous connection between the ownership of HK Investments and owners of casinos on Macau. Nothing of substance. There's not even a valid reason to end negotiations in respect to the Pacific Property Edward Street deal!'

Max could see that Jackson was frustrated, but acknowledged that he was correct. There wasn't anything of substance they could take to the authorities. 'Let's see what Jennifer Armitage says. The meeting is only ten minutes away. I've arranged to meet Jennifer downstairs and bring her up in the goods lift. It exits on the reception level below us adjacent to the secure door that leads to the meeting room I have booked. I've informed Jess on reception that I have a very important client meeting and plan to take the client directly to the meeting room. Even if she sees us arrive, Jess will only see the back of Jennifer.'

'Thanks, Max. I knew you'd have a plan.'

'Have to be careful these days with deadshits like Everingham and Fletcher around. I'd better head off. I'll buzz you from the meeting room when we get there. You come down the internal fire stairs, as we usually do, and I'll leave the two of you alone when you get there. You can buzz me when it's over, and we can reverse the process. That way no one will know it was you who met with the client, and not me.'

Chapter 63

Max had selected the meeting room well and scoped out the logistics of what he had described perfectly. He left the room promptly as soon as Jackson arrived.

'I'm very sorry about Ian,' said Tom to Jennifer Armitage.

'Thanks, Tom.' Jennifer was struggling to maintain her composure. 'I can't believe Ros is gone too. What the hell is happening?'

'We've got all the time we need so let's compare notes and decide where to from here.' Tom didn't know Jennifer very well and was uncertain if he could trust her in this. At the very least she would have to explain her reactions at last week's board meetings.

As if she had read his mind, Jennifer started with the board meetings. 'My role in the two Pacific board meetings last week must have you wondering if you can trust me.'

Jackson was impressed with her perceptiveness yet he simply nodded and signalled for her to continue. Jennifer spent some time detailing everything relating to her role at Pacific, starting with the approach from Ros and Richard, and the call a few months later from James Yeo.

'I recall what Richard said in last Thursday's board meeting about your relationship with James Yeo, and I must admit I was surprised,' Jackson interrupted. 'I hadn't appreciated that you had been reporting information to him for several months. What exactly did you tell him?'

'It all seemed pretty harmless at first,' Jennifer admitted. 'I know it was not the right thing to do, but Yeo said that he had a role in the deal, and that our contact had been sanctioned by Richard Black. I should have checked with Richard. He also led me to believe that he had me in mind for other board positions in the industry, and you know how well-connected and respected he is. Initially I provided weekly updates with very basic information, which did not seem to be of any significance, particularly once it was confirmed that he had a role in arranging finance for the Pacific–HKI deal. Things began to change though when I called James Yeo after the board meeting on Monday last week to tell him of your planned investigation.'

She had Jackson's attention now. He wanted to yell at her, but chose to simply nod and invite her to continue. He wanted her to tell him everything she knew.

'Things escalated after I spoke with Richard Black once I had been notified of Thursday's out-of-sequence board meeting. I told him about James Yeo. He was quite dismissive and wanted to be sure I had not told anyone else. In fact, he insisted that I did not tell Ros Green about it. You heard what Richard said in the Thursday meeting. He said that he had known about, and had approved, my contact with James Yeo. I suspected that may not have been the case and couldn't figure out why he was covering for me.'

Jackson and Ros had suspected that Richard Black was involved, and Jennifer's information did nothing to dissuade him from that view. 'Continue please, Jennifer.'

'I confronted Richard after Thursday's meeting. He told me he was covering for me, and hoped that what he had said would throw you off the trail of my relationship with James Yeo. He seemed particularly upset when I raised the issue of casino ownership and threatened me when I mentioned I would have to talk to Ian about this. Oh Tom, I didn't mean to say out loud that I needed to talk to Ian. Do you think I had something to do with Ian's death?'

'But Ian's death was an unfortunate accident, wasn't it?' pressed Jackson.

'No way. Ian was an excellent driver, and he knew both the road and the limits of his Porsche exceptionally well.' Jennifer proceeded to tell Jackson much the same as she'd told his estranged wife over coffee on Sunday. He was starting to think that he could trust her after all. Jackson thought of it as a bond formed out of adversity, not unlike the bond he and Max had formed all those years ago to deal with insecure and selfish elements in the partnership.

Jackson decided to tell Jennifer what happened in London, and how he was absolutely certain that Ros had been killed. He held back the information about James Yeo's rumoured gambling debt, for now.

Chapter 64

Max Grenfell quietly opened the door to the meeting room, delivered two double-shot cappuccinos and turned to leave. 'Thought you two may need these about now. Everything okay?'

Jackson and Jennifer both nodded their appreciation to Max as he left.

'So here we are,' Tom said. 'Caught in the middle of what could be a serious attempt by criminals to launder a significant amount of money. As soon as we begin sniffing around, bad things start to happen. Two wonderful people are dead, and we both think that neither fatality was an accident nor a suicide. As I said to Max this morning, we can't prove anything, and therefore can't yet go to the authorities. We don't even have enough information to forcefully suggest to the board of Pacific that it break off negotiations with HKI.'

'Until now,' Jennifer said, almost triumphantly.

'You have my undivided attention, Jennifer. What have you discovered?'

Jennifer produced a brief report and explained that Ian's colleague, Ray Kean, had handed it to her yesterday. 'Ray and I met last Saturday and agreed that we owed it to Ian to follow up on the enquiries he initiated on the morning of his horrible accident.'

Jackson read the report and quickly concluded that the information it contained was significant. 'How good are the people who sourced this information?'

'Ray tells me they are the best,' said Jennifer. 'He and Ian are, or at least Ian was, sorry, at the top of their game. I understand they have used these particular investigators on many occasions, and with great success.'

The report established that the two Cayman Island entities were in fact owned by the same parties, proving a direct connection between the ownership of HK Investments and casinos in Macau.

'I don't know how Ian's investigators were able to break down the usually impenetrable barriers in the Caymen Islands, but I'm not sure I want to. If this is all correct, it proves that HK Investments is owned by people who also own casinos.' Jackson made another decision while he was talking. 'I need to also tell you something else, which makes the information you've provided even more significant. One of our investigator's sources told him of a rumour that James Yeo has a gambling problem and may owe a huge debt to the operators of an illegal casino in Hong Kong.'

Jennifer's eyes widened 'You mean James Yeo may be heavily involved in this?'

'It sure looks like it,' responded Jackson.

They chatted for a while, agreeing that what they had was not yet sufficient to prove anything, but that they should use it to defer tomorrow's Pacific board meeting for seven days to enable a little more work to be done. Once they had reached an understanding of what each was to do, Jackson arranged for Max to escort Jennifer out of the office.

Chapter 65

Tom Jackson was waiting in Max's office when he returned. 'All sorted. I'm pretty sure no one saw us,' said Max, walking into his office and closing the door. 'How did it go?'

'Thanks, Max. I really appreciate your assistance with this.' Jackson described to Max how the meeting went and what they had agreed to do.

'Smart plan,' said Max with his trademark grin. 'Just be a bit careful about Jennifer. As I've mentioned to you, she doesn't always play by the rules. That said, I agree with you that you do have a common bond to expose the truth.'

As Jackson headed back to his office, he noticed Roger Everingham observing him, but pretending not to. *How did I come to be in partnership with that man,* he thought to himself, not for the first time.

Tom was not sure if Everingham and his sidekick Miles Fletcher had had anything to do with the flow of information about what he was up to. Someone must have been providing information to Richard Black and his partners in crime. Each new lead and direction he sought to pursue was shut down, or terminated almost immediately. He inwardly shuddered. Had these pricks been the ones to alert Richard and others of his and Ros' meeting arrangements in London, or had Ros made that information available to Richard? For now, he had to assume that Everingham was somehow involved as well as Fletcher, and he resolved to minimise paper trails of what he had planned for next week.

Chapter 66

Jennifer Armitage called Kevin Lightfoot, another Pacific board member, as soon as she returned to her office.

'How are you holding up, Jennifer?' Kevin said as he answered the call.

'It hasn't really sunk in yet, but I'm okay, I guess. Thanks for asking. I'm still trying to get my head around the loss of Ian, and now the fact that Ros Green is gone too.' Jennifer was steeling herself.

'It unfortunately shows what a fine line we all tread.' Kevin sounded philosophical.

Yeah, right, thought Jennifer, *especially if you cross the wrong people.* She continued in a pleasant tone. 'I presume that with Ros' departure, you have now assumed the role of Pacific Property Board Chair?'

'Correct,' said Kevin.

'I think we should postpone tomorrow's scheduled board meeting for seven days, until the following Friday.' She could hear Kevin draw breath, as if to talk, but kept speaking to avoid his interruption. 'Hear me out, please Kevin. Poor Ros died on Monday. I think it would be completely inappropriate, and almost disrespectful, for us to hold a board meeting in the same week. Also, when I called Tom Jackson to offer my support to him – the man was standing right next to Ros when it happened – he told me that there was still a little way to go with the documentation negotiation. Nothing of any significance, I understand, but nevertheless fine-tuning of things that require final agreement.'

'I agree with the issue of respect for Ros and, of course, I trust Tom Jackson's judgement implicitly. What I can't understand is why we must defer the meeting for seven days. I'm keen to see this deal across the line, and as I understand it, Tom's investigations have not uncovered anything of verifiable substance to discredit any aspect of it. Why can't we aim for Monday or Tuesday?' Kevin was calm and businesslike.

Verifiable substance, ha, thought Jennifer to herself. 'Tom also mentioned to me that he'll be travelling to Hong Kong to attend a childhood friend's wedding, which he says he absolutely cannot miss. Apparently, it's been planned for some time and Jackson had thought this deal would well and truly be across the line by now. He leaves on Sunday and returns on Thursday. In my view it is essential that Tom Jackson be present at the board meeting to personally deliver his legal sign off on the documentation for the HKI deal.'

'I agree that Tom must be present at the board meeting that is scheduled to approve the deal,' Kevin said, pausing for a moment to reflect on what Jennifer had said. 'He has been through a lot and, to be fair, he would have been entitled to assume that the HKI deal would have been stitched up before his planned trip. Richard will probably hit the roof. He's very protective of his bonus. I'll smooth it over with him. Okay, I agree, Jennifer. I'll talk to Richard and will then circulate a note to directors with the detail of the meeting's deferral.'

Chapter 67

Kevin Lightfoot was right. Richard Black was not happy. He had agreed with George Kim's confident pronouncement that the deal would go ahead tomorrow. Against all odds, they were almost there.

He couldn't argue with the fact that it may be disrespectful to Ros to hold a board meeting so soon after her death. Richard had not been convinced it had been necessary to terminate Ros, but had nevertheless accepted the view that decisive action had been required. After all, there was a lot at stake.

He had reluctantly agreed to allow the seven-day deferral of the board meeting. He'd told Kevin he would insist that everything must be ready by then, and that he would become directly involved in any final negotiations while Jackson was away in Hong Kong.

Hong Kong? he wondered to himself. *Coincidence or not?* He quickly dismissed any thoughts of concern. Jackson would have planned ahead for some time a trip for a longstanding friend's wedding. He knew that weddings in Hong Kong were not spur-of-the-moment events. In any event it was highly unlikely that Jackson would take the risk of undertaking any further investigations so soon after Ros Green's and Ian Fox's accidental deaths.

George Kim had come to much the same view as Richard, who had called him with the update. He too was a little frustrated but reasoned that they had been patient for some time now and should continue to be. 'Tomorrow week it is then.'

Kim had sounded almost happy to Richard.

Neither Richard Black nor George Kim had thought it necessary to tell James Yeo that Jackson was headed for Hong Kong next week. Richard offered to send James an email with notification of the seven-day deferral, however.

Chapter 68

Jackson was exhausted so decided to head home early. He spent a little time with his team discussing outstanding issues with documentation on the Pacific deal. There was nothing of any real significance, and certainly nothing that couldn't be sorted out during his absence next week.

Tom had a great relationship with the lawyers who worked with him. They respected him. As busy as he usually was, he always had time for his team, and was the first to assist in any crisis. His team members were aware of his upcoming trip to Hong Kong for his friend's wedding.

There were several other smaller matters that he had running and he saw that they too were under control.

He was able to quickly deal with his outstanding emails, including the endless administration. There weren't too many he hadn't already seen. Like most at this level of the legal industry, Jackson constantly checked his emails while he was awake, irrespective of the time zone he was in. To do otherwise was dangerous.

On one memorable occasion in the past, Tom had been in a lengthy meeting with a client in Sydney, and so had not been able to take any calls or check his emails. Another partner in his office had swiftly swooped on an urgent series of calls and had intercepted a hotel acquisition deal which a Sydney partner would have preferred to refer to Jackson.

'I'll be working from home tomorrow, Samantha,' he told his PA as he left his office.

'Have a great trip to Hong Kong, Tom. I assume you have already made the travel arrangements?'

'Will do, thanks, and yes.' Jackson hadn't made any travel arrangements for next week yet, but would do so this evening.

Chapter 69

After he'd poured himself a whisky at home, Tom decided to call his estranged wife Mary to thank her for arranging the meeting with Jennifer.

'No problems, Tom. Happy to help. How did the meeting go?'

Very businesslike, thought Tom, sighing inwardly with the feeling that his heart was shrinking a little.

'Much better than expected, thanks.' Jackson gave Mary a brief summary of the meeting, and the strategy he and Jennifer had agreed on.

'Are you sure she can be trusted?' Mary knew the answer to this question, but felt she needed to ask it. Jackson's instincts were usually spot on, but he had been through a lot lately.

'I've thought very carefully about that. As you know, I don't trust many people, and I never trust anyone until they first demonstrate why I should.'

Mary had heard Tom say this on many occasions before. While that was not how she was wired, she knew that he had developed this attitude as a protective mechanism. In his early years of legal practise, he had experienced (and personally suffered from) some very nasty behaviour.

'I have come to the view that it was Jennifer's naivety, and not any measure of dishonesty, which resulted in her involvement. It was obvious to me in our meeting today that she was being honest, and has a vested interest in seeing the truth exposed. You met with her on Sunday. What's your take on her?'

'I agree. She was clearly distraught and is anxious to make things right.'

'I plan to head to Hong Kong on Sunday to confront James Yeo. I need to get to the bottom of this. I'll back on Thursday.' Jackson clenched his fists.

'I understand why you want to do that, but is it really safe for you?'

'I can take care of myself, and I plan to ask Jason Jones to come over for support. I'll get Jason to travel separately and have him stay in a nearby hotel to keep an eye on me. I also think he should come with me to the meeting with James Yeo.'

'Is there an end in sight to all this?' Mary sounded genuinely concerned.

'No doubt in my mind.' Jackson sounded more confident than he felt. 'I believe that if we confront James Yeo, and he confirms the link between his gambling debt and his involvement in the deal, then we can hand it all over to the authorities to deal with. Besides, if we don't do this, Ian and Ros's deaths may have been for nothing.'

Jackson agreed to keep Mary informed and politely ended the call.

Chapter 70

After making the travel arrangements to Hong Kong, Tom called Jason Jones.

'Thanks for arranging Russell to keep me company in London, Jase. Well, he was not very talkative, but you know what I mean. I felt safe.'

'No problems, mate. Glad you made it back to Oz in one piece.'

'I need a real favour,' continued Tom. He told Jason about his meeting with Jennifer this afternoon, and set out the strategy they had each agreed to follow.

'Awesome info, Tom. Fucked if I know how the bean counter's investigators got a hold of that shit, but it gives us something to sink our teeth into. Great plan, too. I agree that if we can link the casino ownership with the gambling debt and Yeo's involvement, we may have the bastards. We'll at least have more than enough to hand over to the cops. Maybe in Honkers as well as Oz. Let's see how that pans out.'

'I'm travelling to Hong Kong on Sunday and back on Thursday. That's enough time to attend a longstanding friend's wedding, including catching up beforehand. It would give me significant comfort if you could tag along and keep an eye on me over there. It might even be a good idea if you accompanied me to the meeting with James Yeo.'

'Gotya covered, mate. Of course I'll come to Hong Kong with you. I like the way you're thinking about Yeo. We need to scare the shit out of him so he fesses up.'

'Thanks, Jason. This really is above and beyond the usual call of duty.'

'All in a day's work, mate.'

Jackson and Jones talked for a while about travel and other logistics. They agreed to meet in Hong Kong on Monday morning, and set up the meeting with James Yeo that day if he was available to see them. Jason had already established that James Yeo would be in his office on Monday, but that didn't mean he would meet with them.

Chapter 71

DAY 12 (Friday)

Jackson's mobile phone rang, but he didn't recognise the number. Whenever he worked from home, he diverted his direct line to his mobile number.

'Tom Jackson.'

'It's Peter Tomlinson.'

He was surprised to hear from Peter and immediately wondered what this call was about.

'Tragic news about Ros.'

'Agreed,' said Jackson cautiously.

'I see the board meeting that was scheduled for today has been postponed until next Friday. I agree with Richard that it would be disrespectful to Ros to hold a meeting this week. He mentioned that there were still a few relatively minor things to negotiate, and that this would take place while you're away on a holiday.' Peter's tone seemed a little sarcastic to Jackson.

'That's correct. It should only take a few days to finalise the documents. As for the holiday, it's to attend a childhood friend's wedding, which has been planned for some time.' Tom still didn't know where this conversation was headed.

'I heard you were going to Hong Kong. Can I assume that your trip has nothing to do with the HK Investments deal?' Peter still sounded a little sarcastic, but maybe that was just his way.

'Absolutely not.' Jackson reminded himself to be very careful here. Had he misconstrued Peter's role in this, or was Peter just being thorough, albeit in a slightly unorthodox manner?

'Okay, fine. I just wanted to make sure that the deal was on track. I understand from Kevin Lightfoot that your investigations have concluded, and that you have not discovered any factual basis on which to discredit any part of the deal. This deal will be transformational for the company, Tom.'

'I understand. I'm sorry about the couple of extra days delay, and am grateful for the board's understanding about my trip.'

'Okay, fine,' Peter said again, and he hung up.

What was that all about? Jackson wondered to himself. *Is he just a difficult individual carrying out his duties as a director in his own way, or does he have some role in this that I have missed completely?* There had been a lot happening lately, and it wouldn't be the first time Jackson had been completely blindsided.

Chapter 72

Day 13 (Saturday)

Jason Jones was one step ahead of Tom Jackson. He knew their strategy was a good one, but was not without risks. They had no way of knowing how James Yeo would react to their unannounced approach, nor what those directing Yeo would do once they found out. It was apparent to Jones that sinister forces were at play here, and that they would stop at nothing to achieve what they had set out to.

Jones thought it best to put in place his contingency plans without informing Jackson. He hoped they would not be needed but didn't want to leave anything to chance.

Jackson would be protected from the moment he arrived in Hong Kong. One of his best mates from the army, Bradley – Brad – Charters, was an expat living on Lantau Island. There were many expat families living on Lantau Island. The Hong Kong International Airport was adjacent to the island, and so not far for Brad to meet up with his team to deploy anywhere in the world on short notice. Hong Kong Island, where Jackson was staying, was a relatively short boat ride away.

Brad had turned his skills as a commando into a very successful international security business, and Jason was aware that Brad had an excellent local team in Hong Kong.

'Brad. Long time no speak,' Jason began his telephone conversation with Charters.

'It has been a while. To what do I owe this unexpected pleasure?'

'I've got a secret squirrel mission for you, mate. I'll be in Hong Kong from late tomorrow until early Thursday. I may have a fucking tiger by the tail, and if so, I'm gonna need some heavy protection.' Jason gave Brad brief details of what was required, but did not divulge exact details of the deal, nor the participants in it. The less people who knew about that the better, at this stage. 'Main thing, mate, is to make sure Tom Jackson is covered at all times while in Hong Kong. Mate's rates too if you can. He's a close friend, and I'm not sure he fully appreciates the potential danger involved.'

'Roger that.' Brad understood clearly what was required of him. He had plenty of resources at his disposal and could easily redirect some of them to cover the roles that he and his best local operatives had been lined up for during the week ahead. Fortunately, much of his work of late had been in and around China.

Brad and Jason chatted for a while about their respective businesses and life in general.

Immediately after he had completed his call with Jason, Brad conference-called the operatives he had in mind. They were to work on a rotation basis, ensuring that at all times there were at least two of them covering Jackson. He explained that Jason would not be far away and may also need assistance. Hopefully none of them would, but Brad told them that they would need to be prepared for anything. 'I understand there have already been a couple of accidental deaths, carried out very professionally. So watch your six.'

Chapter 73

Day 14 (Sunday)

Roger Everingham was not happy. He had been unable to provide any more information to James Yeo since the revelations Miles Fletcher had discovered the previous Saturday. Even worse still, Yeo had completely ignored Roger all week.

Everingham had seen Jackson meeting with Max Grenfell during the week, but they always did that. Miles had kept a careful eye on time-recorded entries by Jackson and his team on the Pacific file, but nothing out of the ordinary had appeared.

He knew that Jackson was away in Hong Kong for most of the week, but all he had been able to find out by his not-so-subtle questioning around the office was that Jackson was attending an old friend's wedding. *Fascinating*, he thought to himself. *There must be more to the trip than that, surely?*

Roger had persuaded Miles Fletcher to come in to the office again on the weekend, this time on a Sunday, to see if he could access anything of use via Jackson's PA's computer user account.

Fletcher had not been too happy about it, but was still keen to ensure that he provided Roger with what he needed. He couldn't afford to lose any friends. He didn't have many.

Miles Fletcher had to spend a significantly larger amount of time on Samantha Brown's user account than last time. It was as if Jackson had known something was up. There was hardly any email traffic on his private email, and nothing in respect to either the Pacific Property deal, or, oddly enough, even his trip to Hong Kong. Miles was smart enough to realise that this needed to be the last time he did this. So far as he was aware, he had escaped detection so far.

Roger Everingham was not, however, too pleased with Miles when he called him to not only tell him he'd found nothing of use, but to also advise that this was the last time he would break into Jackson's work or private email account.

'That's fascinating, but I think you're wrong.' Roger's attempt at sounding knowledgeable failed miserably. 'There is no way Tom could have twigged to the fact that you've hacked his email accounts, Miles. Thanks for trying again today, eh. Let's do it again some time.'

Miles had no intention of checking Jackson's emails that way again. He was far more risk averse than Everingham. 'We'll see,' was all he said to Roger, as a parent would to a child who didn't really understand that the debate had now ended.

Chapter 74

Jackson's flight arrived on time, shortly after 5:00 p.m. Hong Kong time. He made his way quickly through immigration and, after collecting his bags, customs and excise control.

On his way to the train station to catch the Airport Express to Hong Kong Central, Tom caught sight of Jason Jones out of the corner of his eye. Jason, who had arrived earlier on a separate flight, had intentionally let himself be seen as a means of reassuring Tom that everything was proceeding as planned. He knew his friend had placed himself in harm's way but was confident that he could take care of himself. He nevertheless took quiet comfort from knowing he had backup if he needed it.

What Jackson didn't know was that both Bradley Charters and his number one operative, Bing Long, were also boarding the same train. Jason was aware that at least one of the pair would be shadowing them, but he hadn't seen either, nor anyone else who appeared to be observing Jackson.

While on the train, Jackson willed himself to relax a little. He needed to have his wits about him for what lay ahead and was already starting to configure his thoughts about tomorrow's meeting with James Yeo. He would refine them overnight and during his discussion with Jason in the morning. In Jackson's mind there was no such thing as over-preparation. He knew that meetings such as these could not be scripted, and that a comprehensive preparation was the best means of being able to coherently deal with any unpredictable direction the meeting may take.

As he arrived at Central and made his way from the train to the nearby taxi rank, Jackson thought he caught sight of someone watching him. Or was it just his imagination? He knew Jason was somewhere nearby, and sincerely hoped he was as good as he was reputed to be on the personal protection side of his business.

Chapter 75

Even though it was Sunday evening, the traffic was still quite heavy. Jackson headed for the start of the long queue of familiar red taxis. The red taxis operated throughout most of Hong Kong. Green taxis only serviced the new territories, and the blue ones only operated on Lantau Island.

Brad Charters and Bing Long saw that Jason was also heading to the taxi rank, and thought he would most likely catch the next taxi. Brad assessed the situation quickly. 'Jason has him covered on the ride to the hotel. With that traffic it could take them around fifteen minutes to get there. Rather than attracting any unnecessary attention at this end or the other, I suggest we jog through Hong Kong Park. We should be able to get there before them.'

'I was thinking much the same thing,' responded Bing.

After observing Jackson load his luggage into a taxi and hop into the back seat, the two of them quietly slipped away from the crowd and began to jog towards the park in the direction of Pacific Place, where Jackson's hotel, the Island Shangri-La, was located.

Chapter 76

Jackson had stayed at the Shangri-La when he and Mary last visited Hong Kong. It was a beautiful five-star hotel with fifty-seven levels. Jackson had requested an upper floor, and wasn't disappointed when he opened the door to his room on Level 48. The room faced Victoria Harbour and he had an unobstructed view across to Kowloon Bay.

He decided to rug up a little and head out for a walk in Hong Kong Park before it got too late. He was thinking that the twilight would provide excellent light for some photos. One of the many hobbies he and Mary had shared was that they enjoyed taking photos on their compact digital cameras, which were so sophisticated these days.

Just to be cautious before heading out, he decided to give Jason a quick call. 'Hey Jase, good trip?'

'Not as good in cattle truck, mate, as where you and the other toffs sat, but good enough. Everything okay?'

'It's probably nothing, but I thought I may have seen someone else following me at Central,' Jackson said apprehensively.

'All good, mate. I mentioned to you that I'd arranged some backup over here, just in case. There's a couple of operatives who will shadow both of us while we're here. A mate of mine has a bloody successful private security business over here and has allocated himself and a few others to the task of protecting us. They'll do it on a rotation basis so that there are at least two of them on the case at any one time, twenty-four seven. Who knows what these fuckers might get up to once they get wind of why you're really here. I was gonna tell you in the morning, but thought I should now, since you may have seen one of them. They're bloody good. I've seen my mate Brad, only because I know him, but I haven't seen the other fella.'

'How do I know if the person I saw is friendly or not?' asked Jackson.

'As I said, these guys are the best. They're all ex-military special forces. They'll know a hostile when they see one, and will make damn sure they don't get to either of us.'

Jones was enjoying this, Jackson realised. 'Just how will they do that?'

'Best you don't know, mate.'

'Okay, thanks, and understood.' Tom was well aware of what he had placed himself in the midst of. He was not one to take unnecessary risks but deep inside he was hoping for an opportunity to vent some of his pent-up anger. That said, he knew the enemy were playing for keeps. 'I'm glad you're over here with me, Jase.'

'No worries, mate.'

'I'm planning a walk in Hong Kong Park shortly while there's still some light. Do you think that's okay?' Jackson asked.

'That's fine, mate. We'll keep an eye on you. It's pretty safe generally in the city, but I reckon you shouldn't stay out too late.'

'I'll head off in about ten minutes.'

'Roger that.'

Chapter 77

The park was spectacular, and the light was superb for photos. Jason Jones saw that there were many other tourists and locals doing exactly the same thing as Tom, taking advantage of the twilight.

Jones intercepted his colleague Brad for a brief chat in the shadows. Bing wandered on so as not to attract any attention. Jason had not seen Brad for several years. 'You're in good shape, mate,' he said.

'Have to be, Jason. Tough game this, especially when you don't have all the information. Never know what to expect.'

'Sorry, buddy. You know how it works. Sometimes it's best to keep things tight. Just wanted to let you know that in the morning we plan to arrange a meet with someone in the Bank of China Tower. Things will get a bit hairy if word gets out about the meeting.'

'Roger that. Thanks for the heads up.' Brad quietly slipped away.

Chapter 78

DAY 15 (Monday)

Tom Jackson and Jason Jones met as agreed in the small business centre meeting room in Jackson's hotel shortly after breakfast. It was a private room on the mezzanine level. They had both arrived separately.

'Other than for Brad and one of his offsiders, I don't believe anybody else is observing you, Tom.' Jason had scoped out Jackson's hotel since early morning.

'That's good news for once.' Tom was a little apprehensive about the potential meeting with James Yeo. 'Let's get on with it.'

Jackson called James Yeo's office on speaker phone. The room they were in was relatively soundproof and there were no adjacent offices, so neither Jackson nor Jones thought they were taking any unnecessary risk. They had agreed that only Tom would speak, and that he would not let James know that anyone else was listening in. This went against Jackson's usual practice. One of his pet hates was when someone called you on speaker phone and failed, intentionally or otherwise, to disclose that somebody else was also in the caller's room. But this meeting was different of course, Tom reminded himself.

'James. This is Tom Jackson from Ridgeway Mason.'

'How are you, Tom? I see we are getting very close to signing up the Pacific Property transaction. Next Friday I believe.' Yeo sounded confident.

'That's correct, James. We'll all be relieved when this one gets over the line. I'm in Hong Kong to celebrate a longstanding friend's wedding and I wondered if we could meet briefly today to discuss a couple of issues relating to the deal? Apologies for the short notice' Tom's voice did not betray the apprehension he felt. Jason was nodding at his performance so far.

The longer-than-necessary pause from James Yeo told both Jackson and Jones that Yeo had not expected Tom to be in Hong Kong. 'I didn't know you were coming to Hong Kong, Tom. Does Richard Black know you're here?'

Tom and Jason looked at each other at the mention of Richard Black's name. *We're closing in on you.* Tom leaned closer to the phone.

'Sure does,' said Jackson casually. 'This is a private holiday trip for me, and is not the cause of the delay in the Pacific board meeting to next Friday. There are still a few documentary negotiations to be finalised, and my team has that well in hand. All concerned also shared the view that it would be a little insensitive to Ros' memory to hold a board meeting in the same week she tragically took her own life. I'm sure you've heard of this by now.' It angered Tom to have to describe Ros' death in this manner, but it was critical that James Yeo did not suspect any ulterior motive behind his request for a meeting with him.

'I agree with you about Ros. I was very sorry to hear that news.' Yeo's sympathy was genuine. Tom and Jason shared another look as if to acknowledge that his tone confirmed their understanding of his role in this.

'There are a couple of issues that I think it best we discuss face to face if for no other reason than to personally meet. We have dealt with each other on several occasions, but have yet to meet in person.' Jackson knew that Asian businessmen preferred to deal with you face to face, at least in the first instance. It was their way of looking into your eyes and assessing if they could trust you.

'I'm free at noon,' Yeo offered. He was well aware of Tom Jackson's reputation and skill, and indicated it would be beneficial to personally meet the man. 'I'm on level 38 of the Bank of China Tower.'

'I know it,' said Jackson. 'Thanks, James. I'll see you then.'

Jason gave Tom the thumbs up as he ended the call. They talked briefly about the meeting before parting company. They would meet in the foyer of Yeo's building shortly before midday.

Chapter 79

James Yeo put the receiver down and thought about the call from Jackson. He had no reason to suspect that Tom had anything in mind other than a personal meeting. He had said that Richard Black was aware, and therefore James had to assume that George Kim also knew that Jackson was in Hong Kong.

That said, there was too much at stake here for Yeo to leave anything to chance. He dialled George Kim's mobile number. 'George, it's James.'

'Yes, I see that. What can I do for you?'

'Did you know Tom Jackson would be in Hong Kong this week?'

'Yes.'

James didn't like George Kim at all, but he had learnt through his dealings with him to proceed with caution. 'Any reason you or Richard didn't inform me?'

'We saw no need to. It's just a holiday as I understand it. What's this about, James?' George sounded like he was starting to lose his patience, something he had precious little of.

'He's coming to see me in a couple of hours,' James continued.

Kim paused before responding. 'Did he say what about?'

'Mainly that he wanted to meet me face to face, and that there were a couple of issues with the Pacific deal he wanted to discuss. I'm sure it's nothing, but I know how important this deal is to all of us, so just wanted to let you know.' Yeo agreed to call Kim after the meeting to let him know what it was about.

*

George Kim ended the call and sat for a moment considering the possibilities. He understood the need to meet face to face, particularly if James Yeo and Tom Jackson hadn't yet had the opportunity to do so. He was confident there was nothing to worry about but he didn't want to make the mistake of underestimating Jackson. He dialled Murray Jensen's number. 'I know it's late, Murray but what resources do you have in Hong Kong?'

'I have multiple resources. What do you need?' Jensen was checking his electronic asset allocation schedule as he was talking.

'I may not need anything at all. On the other hand, I may need decisive action, quickly, depending on what transpires at a meeting in Hong Kong at midday today.'

'Call me when you know. In the meantime, I'll re-task a couple of assets to be on standby.' Jensen knew it would be very early in the morning London time when he next heard from George Kim, but also knew that the adrenaline surge he got from each new job would prevent him from sleeping.

Kim provided a few essential details of the location of the meeting and participants before he ended the call. *Best to be prepared for any eventuality*, he thought. *We're much too close to let anything get in our way.*

Chapter 80

'How well do you know James Yeo?' George Kim had decided to call Richard Black to inform him of recent developments, and to see if he could assist with assessing the risks that might flow from the scheduled meeting between Yeo and Jackson.

'No better than you, I'm sure. Why, what's up?' Richard was immediately on alert.

'Tom Jackson has set up a meeting shortly with James Yeo. James says he thinks it's just to take the opportunity to meet face to face, but I'm not so sure. Jackson is not one to be underestimated. I've taken the liberty of involving Murray Jensen. He will have local assets on standby just in case.' George Kim did not seem at all concerned at the prospect of once again involving hired killers.

Richard knew what may have to be done, but that didn't mean he had to like it. 'It goes without saying that Murray's assets should not be deployed unless they absolutely have to be.'

'So why say it.' Kim's quick and somewhat aggressive response reminded Richard that the man did not take too kindly to having his judgement questioned. 'How much do you think James has been able to piece together?'

'As far as I'm aware, he would have no idea that the funds for the deal are sourced from the same businesses to which he is indebted to.' Richard said. 'I'm sure if he has turned his mind to it, he would have wondered at the coincidental timing, but I can't imagine any way he would have been able to procure proof of the connection. In any event, he's on the same team as us, at least for now. He is well aware of the personal risks he faces if his gambling debt remains unpaid for much longer. Why would he rock that boat?'

'I agree with you.' Kim was sounding calmer now. 'I just wanted to get a second opinion.'

Chapter 81

Jason Jones had been waiting outside and followed Jackson into the foyer of the Bank of China Tower. He lightly touched Tom on the elbow and subtly steered him towards the lift bank. Jason knew that the less time he and Jackson were seen in public together the better.

They had been seen, however. Andrew Wong was the head of Muray Jensen's operations in Hong Kong. He had been waiting for Tom Jackson to arrive for his scheduled meeting at midday, and had been surprised to see another man accompany him to the lift. Thinking quickly, he had been able to take a digital photo of the second man's profile. It wasn't great, but it was better than nothing. He decided to transmit it to Murray Jensen immediately to see if he could identify the other person.

There were others in the lift, preventing Tom and Jason from discussing anything important. Neither was concerned. They had been over this thoroughly, and each trusted the other.

They were the only ones to exit when the lift stopped at level 38.

'Tom Jackson to see James Yeo,' Jackson said to the female receptionist.

'Mr Yeo was only expecting you, Mr Jackson. Who may I tell him is the other person.'

Her English was excellent, Tom thought. 'This is my colleague, Neil Frawley. Please tell James that Neil has been advising on local law aspects of the Hong Kong-sourced finance for the Pacific deal that James and I are to discuss.' Jackson noticed that the receptionist had written down much of what he'd said.

She spoke quietly into her headset in mandarin. 'Mr Yeo will see you now, gentlemen. Follow me please.'

They were led into a conference room with a magnificent view of Victoria Harbour. The receptionist closed the door as she left.

Chapter 82

It wasn't long before the conference room door opened and an immaculately dressed Chinese man walked in. Yeo was a very youthful-looking forty-eight- year-old man with neatly clipped black hair that had distinctive grey streaks throughout. He was lean but not tall. He wore a tailored navy suit with a subtle black pinstripe, a white shirt and a blood-red tie.

'James Yeo,' he said with an outstretched hand for Tom to shake. 'Pleased to finally meet you in person, Tom.'

Jackson shook his hand. 'Likewise, James. I feel I know you well, but you never really know someone until you meet them.'

Yeo hesitated momentarily before turning his attention to Jason. 'I wasn't expecting anyone else. Neil Frawley, I understand.'

'That's right,' said Jason, trying unsuccessfully to sound less Australian than he was. 'I've been assisting Tom with aspects of this deal.'

'Funny,' said Yeo. 'Your name hasn't come up before.'

Jackson quickly stepped in. 'Do you mind if we sit, James?'

'Of course. Please sit on that side and enjoy the wonderful view.' Yeo's Chinese–American accent was very familiar to Jackson.

'Thank you for seeing us on such short notice,' began Tom.

'My absolute pleasure. It's great to finally meet the famous Tom Jackson.'

'Likewise. Your reputation precedes you.' Jackson intentionally zeroed in on Yeo's reputation. He knew that James had been born and schooled in Hong Kong, and had gained his tertiary education at an

American-run university. Reputation preservation would be sacrosanct to him.

'You are most kind.' Yeo slightly bowed his head.

With the usual pleasantries out of the way, Jackson got straight to the point. 'My friend here is assisting us with the Pacific deal, but not in the traditional sense you might expect. Sorry to slightly mislead you, but it is critical that you know the truth.'

'I'm listening.'

James seemed calm. Tom thought he might know what was to come. Everyone knew by reputation alone that his integrity was beyond reproach.

Jackson took a deep breath. 'We have established that HK Investments is owned by the same entities which own casinos in Macau.' Yeo nodded for Tom to continue.

'We know for sure you owe a lot of dosh to an illegal casino operating right here in Hong Kong.' Coming from Jason, this had the desired effect of shocking Yeo, and he was momentarily off balance.

'But how did you...?' Yeo stopped himself from saying any more, but he didn't need to.

'You've been used, mate.' Jason looked as if he wanted to say more but Jackson silenced him with a small wave of his hand. They had planned this, but hadn't expected to get an admission from Yeo so easily.

So far so good, thought Jackson. 'We're not here to trap you, James.' Jackson's tone was conciliatory. Inwardly he felt some sympathy for this man. He had worked very hard for his achievements and it was all about to be undone. At the same time, Tom also felt angry and conflicted by the outrageous consequences of the unfolding events that Yeo was connected to.

'Then why are you here?' Yeo was starting to rebuild his defences.

'To expose the truth. Two innocent people are dead, and we believe they were killed by the people who are manipulating you.'

Yeo involuntarily winced when Jackson said the word manipulating. This did not go unnoticed by either Jackson or Jones. Instinctively, they both knew they were on the right track.

Chapter 83

Jackson spent some time describing to James Yeo the untimely deaths of both Ian Fox and Ros Green.

Yeo reflected on this information for a moment. 'But Ian's death sounds like an accident, and Ros's was by her own hand. From what you say, the investigators have independently concluded there was nothing suspicious in either death. Coincidental I know, but an accident and a suicide nonetheless.'

'You don't believe that, James, and neither do we.' Jackson thought it was time to lay it all out for James Yeo. 'As we see it, you have amassed a huge unpaid gambling debt to the operators of an illegal casino in Hong Kong. The owners of the illegal operation also own legitimate casinos on Macau.

'I have been aware for some time now of attempts to launder a huge amount of funds by way of property-related transactions in Australia. It's why I insisted to Pacific Property's board that we investigate the source of funds.'

Yeo looked as if he wanted to interrupt Jackson.

'Hear me out please, James. $750 million is a huge amount of money to be lent on the one deal. That alone raised my suspicions. As soon as I became aware of the disproportionate returns to HK Investments and Pacific Property, I knew I had to dig deeper.

'The harder we looked the more difficult it became, and the serious and very regrettable consequences I have already described to you began to unfold.

'James, you may not have intended it, but you have been manipulated and now you are implicated in the deaths of two innocent people. Those who are directing you will stop at nothing to see this deal over the line.'

Jackson's last comments had a serious effect on James Yeo, and he lowered his eyes in shame. He was silent for some time, and Jackson and Jones knew that they should wait for him to digest what had been said.

Yeo slowly raised his head. 'It was probably naïve of me to think that it was coincidental luck.'

Jackson and Jones remained silent as he continued.

'Your information is correct. I have finally admitted to myself that I have an issue with gambling. It wasn't enough that I could go to any one of many legal casinos. I had to get involved with an illegal one on Hong Kong Island. I thought my luck would eventually turn.' Yeo appeared to be almost talking to himself, although he looked up at the two men before continuing.

'I owe five million, and significant pressure is being applied for repayment. I should have guessed that the promise of a personal 1% ($7.5 million) commission for raising the $750 million finance for the Pacific deal was far too convenient. It was an opportunity I knew I had to take. I had no way of repaying the debt and was starting to have concerns for my own safety. I never intended for this to happen.'

Jackson could see that James Yeo was clearly distraught. But Tom was inwardly seething. Yeo was still involved in a series of events that had led to the tragic and completely unnecessary deaths of two wonderful people, including one he cared deeply about.

With an effort, he forced himself to remain calm. There was too much at stake.

'I understand, James. We find ourselves in these positions incrementally. It's only with the clarity of hindsight that we can sometimes see the awful consequences of our actions. This is one of those times.'

James was nodding his agreement.

Jackson continued. 'There is a way to make this right.'

Yeo knew exactly what Jackson was asking. 'But my reputation will be ruined.' He knew as soon as he said this that it already was.

Chapter 84

Without saying another word, Yeo stood up and moved to a painting on an inner wall. He slid the painting sideways to reveal a small wall safe. Jason Jones tensed a little, alert for what might happen.

Utilising the iris scanner and thumb print twin security, the Chinese man opened the safe and withdrew an A4-sized manila folder. Jason was relieved to see that there was nothing else in the safe, and he relaxed a little.

Yeo gently placed the folder in front of him as he sat down. He stared at the folder for some time before sliding it across to Jackson. 'I know I have done the wrong thing but I never imagined consequences such as you have described.'

The man was almost trance-like. 'I trust you, Tom. I have had my suspicions for some time, and have done a little investigating of my own. Please have a look through the information and documents in the folder and ask me any questions.'

Jackson moved the folder between he and Jones, and together they looked through its contents, glancing up at each other from time to time. Neither knew whether to be happy or sad, but each knew that the information James had provided, when combined with what Jason and Ian Fox's colleague had uncovered, was more than sufficient to go to the authorities in both Hong Kong and Australia.

Tom looked at Jason and shook his head. 'We have no questions at the moment, James. What you have given us establishes the existence of the illegal casino, and locates it. It will also direct the authorities to at least some of those involved. You do realise this seriously implicates you in a number of illegal activities, not the least of which is an undisclosed significant commission. I am surprised to see that it was you who initially directed the application of pressure on me. Did you also direct the other activities that resulted in the deaths of Ian Fox and Ros Green?' Jackson was outwardly angry now.

James looked shocked. 'No! I admit I did, somewhat reluctantly, direct the application of pressure on you, but I had nothing to do with either of the fatalities. That is not my way. I expect it will have been George Kim, whom I have never met, and whose contact details you now have, who directed this.'

What exactly is your way? Jackson thought to himself. He quickly realised that he needed Yeo for now, and he shelved the revulsion he was feeling towards this man. 'How would you like us to proceed from here?'

James Yeo knew that he was finished. He knew what he had to do. Returning his mind to the present he said, 'Completely your call, Tom. I'm in your hands. I just want to make it right.'

They talked amongst themselves for a while. Tom and Jason were able to more completely verify the sources of Yeo's information, and between them they filled in a few missing components. At Yeo's insistence they also prepared a statement for him to sign in front of them. Neither of them understood why he insisted on doing this, but they were certain that the statement would be invaluable in the next steps.

Yeo took two copies of all the documents and placed one set in his safe. He gave the originals and the other set of copies to Jackson, hesitantly at first. Then, as if he'd made his mind up about something he had been contemplating, Yeo shook Jackson's hand firmly, looked him directly in the eyes and said, 'I trust you. Please make this right, and be careful. These people are ruthless.'

Chapter 85

With mixed feelings, they left the meeting. Tom kept the originals, and Jason the copies. To their surprise, they had been in the meeting with James for more than two hours.

They were alone on their way down in the lift.

'Holy shit, mate. This stuff's serious and could get someone killed. We need to get this to those who should know pronto.'

They headed to a nearby café and selected a private booth towards the rear. Both were in need of some sustenance, and needed somewhere private to discuss what they would do next.

Andrew Wong was waiting outside and saw the pair leave together. Murray Jensen had not been able to identify Jones from the photo Andrew had sent through to him earlier, and had asked him to try for a better shot. To do this, Andrew had to move out of the shadows a little, and the act of raising his camera immediately attracted the attention of both Brad Charter and Bing Long, who had also been waiting for Jackson and Jones to emerge from their meeting.

Brad immediately pinged Jason's phone with a prearranged signal. Jason had seen the signal on the way to the café and knew instantly that Brad had detected a potential danger. He called Brad from the café. 'What's up, mate?'

'You have a tail. He took a photo of you both as you came out of the Bank of China Tower.' Brad sounded concerned.

'Recognise him?' Jason said quickly.

'No, but until he moved to take the photo, we hadn't noticed him at all, so I expect he's a professional. How'd the meeting go, and what's next?' Brad asked

'Shit.' Jason was thinking fast now. 'That means others knew about our meeting. We have information that they would kill to retrieve. Do you have somewhere secure nearby we could meet to put a plan together?'

Brad gave Jason directions to a secure apartment he kept in Central Hong Kong for this type of eventuality. It was only two blocks away. 'I'll have Bing ensure that your shadow is disengaged.'

'Roger that. See you there in ten.' Jones ended the call. He didn't need to know anything else.

'Let's go.' Jason stood up abruptly. 'I'll explain on the way.'

Tom knew better than to second guess Jason and followed him out of the café.

Chapter 86

Andrew Wong was surprised to see the pair exit the café they had only just entered. As he made to follow them, a very strong arm grabbed him around the throat and drew him back into the shadows. He moved to struggle but thought better of it when he felt a metal object press painfully into his back.

'It is what you think it is, so don't make a fuss,' Bing snarled into Andrew's ear.

A van arrived and Bing pushed Wong inside where he was quickly and efficiently restrained by others from Brad's team.

In less than a minute, Andrew Wong had been disengaged as Brad had promised, and Bing had signalled confirmation to Brad.

Brad was glad he'd arranged for a mobile backup team to be on hand. He didn't know exactly what was going on, but he knew enough to warrant abundant caution.

Chapter 87

Andrew Wong had managed to transmit a slightly better photo of Jason Jones to Murray Jensen before he was apprehended.

Jensen was running the photo through his extensive database and thought he would also send it to George Kim to see if he knew the man.

Kim received the photo together with a note that this was taken as Jackson and the man in question had emerged from their meeting with James Yeo. That meant the meeting went for over two hours. James should have called him by now, and who was the second person? He did not recognise him, but perhaps Richard Black would.

George Kim thought he would give James Yeo a little more time to call, and instead called Richard Black. 'Jackson spent over two hours with James Yeo, and a second man was with him. I'm sending you a photo now.'

Richard took the phone away from his ear to view the photo 'Shit. That's Jason Jones from JJ Investigations. He's the one who's been investigating our deal for Jackson. Why on earth is he in Hong Kong, and what the hell is he doing accompanying Jackson to a meeting with James Yeo?'

'I need to ring James Yeo right now.' Kim ended the call.

Chapter 88

'James Yeo, please.' George Kim was annoyed that Yeo hadn't called him yet, but didn't let it show.

'I'm afraid Mr Yeo has left the office, and I'm unsure of when he will return. Can I take a message.' Kim had already ended the call.

He called Murray Jensen. 'The photo you sent me is of Jason Jones, an investigator Jackson has hired to look into aspects of a deal we are working on. Richard Black recognised him. Jackson and Jones spent over two hours in the meeting I mentioned. Much longer than I expected, and Jones was not supposed to have been there. My contact at the meeting has not called me as he said he would, and is now unavailable. Jackson may have information we don't want him to. At the very least, I need to retrieve any information Tom was given in the meeting.'

'Do you have anything specific in mind, and are there any limits you would like to impose on our actions?' Jensen was still trying to understand how he had lost contact with his senior operative, Andrew Wong, and needed a little more time to think about it.

'Let's avoid termination for now, at least until we know exactly what we're dealing with.' Kim knew the line to be secure, and so had no issues with being direct. 'There has been enough bloodshed, and too many accidents with possibly the same common denominator, our deal, will be difficult for the authorities to dismiss without further detailed investigation. We don't want that. Just find out what information Yeo gave them and report back. We can decide what to do then.'

Murray Jensen had decided not to tell Kim just yet that he may have lost contact with his Hong Kong operative. There may be a perfectly logical explanation for his lack of contact. He decided instead to task another key asset to locate Wong, or at least pick up his trail. They knew where Jackson was staying. It should not be too difficult to locate the pair and ask Tom politely what he'd learnt at the midday meeting. His team was good at that.

Chapter 89

James Yeo tidied his desk after the meeting with Jackson and Jones, swivelled his chair around and enjoyed his view of Victoria Harbour. After a few moments' contemplation, he left his office without telling his assistant where he was going, just that he didn't know when he'd be back.

As he headed for his nearby high-rise apartment, he felt at peace. He reflected on many things on the way home. He had been incredibly successful, and had well and truly earned the reputation he had in the property finance industry.

Why did I have to throw it all away? he asked himself. *Gambling had just been a hobby, hadn't it? When did it become an obsession?* He had been horrified to hear of the terrible consequences of his actions even though he knew he was not directly responsible for the deaths. As Jackson had said, however, he had certainly been manipulated, and was now implicated in the deaths of two innocent people. As soon as he had heard that, he knew what he must do. He must right the wrong.

Before James Yeo knew it, he had arrived at the luxury building in which he owned one of the two penthouses on level 30. He gave a friendly wave to the concierge in his building and headed to the private lift that serviced only the two penthouses.

James had always loved the view from his penthouse. He often reflected on the high cost of his success: many casual acquaintances, but he had never had sufficient time to commit to a serious relationship, and so had never married. He had been lonely at times, although he loved his work.

He walked out on to his huge deck and stared out over the harbour. It occurred to him that he rarely arrived home before the sun set, and never did so in winter. *What a magnificent city*, he thought as he climbed onto the deck chair he had absentmindedly moved to the railing, and jumped.

Chapter 90

Tom Jackson and Jason Jones arrived at Brad Charters' apartment just before he did. As they all entered the building together and headed for the lift bank, Brad looked around and was satisfied that the foyer was empty. He had intentionally chosen an older apartment block to buy a unit in. One with no reception or concierge. Less eyes to observe, he'd thought.

Brad used his security card to activate the lift. 'Bing has removed your shadow and will remain outside to alert us if anyone else turns up. But I'm sure we weren't followed.'

Just to be absolutely certain Brad called Bing to confirm.

'All good. No tails,' Brad affirmed. 'You will both be safe here for now.

'What do you mean by Bing has removed our shadow?' Jackson was trying to get his head around what was happening, and knew he probably didn't want to know the answer to the question he'd just asked.

'Let's just say Mr Shadow will not be available to bother you while you are in our fair city.' Brad was keen not to disclose his methods.

Jason nodded knowingly, and Tom stared blankly at them. This was not his world, so best leave it to the experts.

Chapter 91

'I've reached need-to-know status, Jason,' said Brad Charters. 'Tell me what's going on so we can work out where to from here.'

Jones looked at Tom, who nodded his assent.

It took a little while for Jason to describe the very recent history of the fast-moving events to Brad. Where necessary, Jackson corrected or added detail. Jason knew most of the details and was very efficient at telling Brad what he had to know.

'Holy shit. You were right, Jason, you do have a tiger by the tail. Neither of you can go back to your hotels. Give me your access keys and room numbers. I'll have my colleagues pack up your gear and we'll discreetly collect it from back of house.' Brad went in to the next room where he could be heard giving short, sharp directions to someone from his team.

When he reappeared, he said, 'We'll need to do this fast, and hopefully before they realise their operative is missing. I'll get it delivered when it's safe to do so. If that can't be done, we'll buy you each some things to get you by until you head back to Australia.'

'Thanks, Jase,' Tom said with obvious relief.

'It's not over yet, Tom.' Jason replied. 'We have enough to nail these bastards. We just have to work out who to give it to. I reckon Brad will be able to help us with the Hong Kong side, although we'll have to be very careful with who we trust. I have some ideas about who to deal with in Oz.'

'Let's hear what Brad has to say before we get too far into who and how.' Jackson was on edge. He was not pleased that he was in this situation. It could, of course, be worse, he reminded himself. Much worse.

Chapter 92

Murray Jensen called Marilyn Turner, who worked closely with Andrew Wong in his Hong Kong office. 'Andrew missed a check-in time. Have you heard from him?' Jensen was beginning to regret not sending the two of them out together. He had instead tasked Andrew to observe and report, and Marilyn had been on standby in their office in Kowloon.

Marilyn was British and had been a star recruit the prior year. She had only recently been sent from Murray's London office to Hong Kong. 'That's not like Andrew. What's your wish?'

Jensen quickly told Marilyn most of what George Kim had just told him. 'Jackson is staying in the Island Shangri-La in Pacific Place. I want you to pick up his trail from there and report in as soon as you sight either him or his investigator Jason Jones.'

'Got it.' Marilyn was ready to move immediately and knew it wouldn't take longer than thirty minutes to arrive at the hotel.

By the time Marilyn arrived, and unbeknownst to her, Brad's people had already removed Jackson's belongings. They had substituted other personal items of clothing and toiletries so it would not be obvious to housekeeping that he was no longer in residence. They had done the same at Jones' nearby hotel.

Chapter 93

Like most people these days, George Kim had set his smart phone to display news alert banners that may be relevant to him. While he received numerous alerts throughout the day, he always took the time to quickly view content as soon as he could.

Kim was stunned to see the banner headline: Prominent Businessman James Yeo has Taken his Own Life. A mild panic came over him as he clicked on the link to read that James had jumped from the balcony of his penthouse. The story went on the say that, while it looked to have been suicide, a crime scene had been established and an investigation was underway.

Kim immediately dialled Murray Jensen's secure line again. 'It's George again, Murray. There's been a disturbing development. The name of the key player at today's midday meeting was James Yeo. I've just seen a media alert that James has committed suicide.'

Jensen was searching for the story as George continued. 'I am now almost certain that James has provided potentially incriminating evidence to Tom Jackson. What's the status of your operation?'

Murray knew it was time to tell George about Andrew Wong. 'I've lost contact with one of my assets and have tasked another to pick up the trail.'

George Kim was fuming. Jensen's reputation and success record were second to none. 'What do you mean, lost contact? We pay you a lot of money, Murray. You know what I expect in return.'

Even though it was winter in London, and very early in the morning, Murray could feel the beads of perspiration begin to form on his forehead. It was not a sensation he had experienced before. 'I'm onto it, George, and will get back to you as soon as we have relocated Jackson.'

*

What the hell was going on? Murray Jensen thought to himself. This was turning out to be far more complex than he imagined. Jones must have arranged local professional assistance for he and Jackson. He couldn't ask Andrew Wong who he thought that might be, and Marilyn Turner was too new to the Hong Kong office to know. He decided to wait for Marilyn to report in and to consider his alternatives in the intervening period. Maybe Andrew would check in.

Chapter 94

Brad Charters ended the call with one of his operatives. 'Your hotel rooms have been cleaned and substitute personal gear installed. That way your early departure won't be detected. We can arrange for you to be formally checked out on Thursday, your scheduled departure date. We were fortunate to get that sorted so quickly. One of our guys thought they saw someone getting in position to observe the front of the Shangri-La. She's either new to the game, or a little unlucky that we spotted her as she arrived. Now we've got that sorted, let's work out what we do from here.'

They talked amongst themselves for over an hour. There were two key issues: How and when should Jackson and Jones return to Australia, and to whom should they give the valuable information they now had?

'It's too dangerous for either of you to remain in Hong Kong.' Brad articulated what each of them was thinking. 'We need to get you out of here tonight before the others, whoever they may be, realise what's happening and mobilise a larger force to apprehend you and take back the information they must now suspect you have.'

'Why do you say they must suspect we have any information?' Jackson asked. 'Sure they know we met with James Yeo, but how could they possibly know he gave us any kind of information.'

'There are two reasons, Tom,' Brad responded. 'The first is that they know you and Jason spent more than two hours with Yeo. That's way more time than is needed for a simple meet and greet, and they would be wondering who Jason was, and why he was at the meeting. The second reason is this.' Brad handed over his mobile phone to Jackson. It displayed the news alert banner on James Yeo's suicide that George Kim had seen.

Jackson clicked on the link to read the story, while Jones looked over his shoulder. He was completely shocked. They all were. 'I certainly didn't expect that outcome.'

'It makes sense, mate,' Jason chimed in. 'It sucks I know, but think about it, Tom. Yeo must have made his mind up about what he was going to do during our meeting with him. It's why he handed over the information so readily. He must have felt shame at what he had become involved with, and knew that his reputation would be rooted. A massive loss of face. I expect he decided that doing himself in was his only way out.'

Brad merely asked them to provide details of their current flight itinerary and set about rearranging their flights.

Chapter 95

In London, Murray Jensen was becoming increasingly concerned. He had not heard from Andrew Wong, and Marilyn Turner had not spotted either Tom Jackson or Jack Jones. It was more than two hours since the meeting with James Yeo had concluded. George Kim would be expecting a report from him soon. What could he tell him?

What would I do if I were Jackson? he thought to himself. If he was given incriminating evidence against someone as powerful as George Kim and his syndicate, he would go to ground until the information had been passed on to the authorities. Would he leave Hong Kong? Probably not. At least not until the information, whatever it was, was passed on to the Hong Kong authorities.

Murray decided to stay the course for now. Jackson must return to his hotel sometime today, mustn't he?

He resolved to wait for Marilyn's next report in around two hours or so before he called George Kim.

Chapter 96

Tom Jackson had been analysing their situation and all of the available information. 'Thanks for reorganising the flights so quickly Brad.'

Brad nodded his acknowledgement.

'Jason is on a separate flight to me and we'll each have a copy of the file provided by James Yeo. It will need to be added to the information that Jason and Ian Fox's colleague have discovered as it provides conclusive evidence to the authorities about what's happening here.

'Jason, please email me your two reports now. The formal one we gave to the board of Pacific, and the other one I know you must have prepared with the additional information that James Yeo's file now confirms is correct.'

Jones was grinning. Of course he had the second report ready.

Tom continued. 'I'll package all of that with what Jennifer Armitage gave me. Brad, do you have office facilities here?'

Brad smiled broadly and led Jackson to another room that Tom had not previously paid much attention to as the door had been closed. Brad opened the door to expose a full suite of office equipment including computers with high-speed internet access and sophisticated printers with copying and scanning capabilities.

Jackson set about compiling the documents and information then stored it on three separate 8GB USB memory sticks that he found in Brad's stationery cupboard. He thought that the cupboard was better stocked than some of the law offices he'd worked in. When he had completed this, Jackson gave a USB to both Jason and Brad. He retained the third USB together with the original documents. Jones also retained the copies Yeo had provided in the meeting.

'We each have a set of the information. If something happens to me, I want you to put this information in the correct hands in Australia. We owe it to Ros and Ian. I've also sent an encrypted set of the information to the private email account of my trusted colleague, Max Grenfell, with strict instructions about what to do with it in the unlikely event that neither Jason nor I can deliver this to the Australian authorities.

'Brad, you know the situation here. Is there anyone senior in the Hong Kong Police Force you trust implicitly and can give this information to? We have to assume that there are police and other public officials engaged in a cover up of the operation of the illegal casino.'

'There are a few people, but one in particular I've known for many years and trust. Money does talk, however, so we will all need to be very careful.' Brad was thinking through the logistics of this.

'We need to leave for the airport in thirty minutes. Your gear has arrived, and my mobile protection unit is downstairs. I like the contingencies you've set up, Tom. Smart thinking. I suggest you don't broadcast to anyone in Australia what you have, except for your colleague Max Grenfell, of course. Do you trust him with your life?' Brad was not taking any chances.

Jackson nodded.

'Good, because that's what you've just done.'

'Once I know the two of you have boarded your flights, I'll go and personally see my contact in the Hong Kong Police Force. As I said, I've known him for years and he was recently promoted to the rank of deputy commissioner. He's been particularly successful at bringing white collar criminals to justice, and I suspect he'll leap at the chance to expose and shut down what must be a significant illegal casino operation.'

'And I know exactly which copper to see when we hit Brisbane.' Jones also sounded confident.

Chapter 97

'Time to leave.' Brad Charters had stood up and headed towards the door. Jackson and Jones were more than ready and followed close behind.

They emerged from the lift in the basement carpark. Brad's mobile unit was waiting. It was a black van with tinted windows.

Bing had confirmed to Brad that he hadn't detected any surveillance of the building they were in. While he'd been told by Brad to take a break, he'd decided to stay on site until his charges were safe.

The door to the van slid open to reveal two huge, muscular men and comfortable seating for six. A third operative was in the driver's seat and the engine was running.

Is this what happened to Mr Shadow? Jackson thought to himself. *Had he been swallowed by this van, and if so, what had subsequently happened to him?* He quickly dismissed any thoughts of sympathy when he remembered that the man had been a threat to his and Jason's safety.

The three of them entered the van, the door was closed, and they headed to the airport. Brad made the introductions. 'Tom, Jason, meet Adam and Brett, and that's Jacqui in the driver's seat. Adam and Jacqui will stay with you at the airport until you board your flights, and Brett and I will come back to the city and await confirmation of departure of both of your flights before we move on to the next phase.'

As if to remind himself of the agreed logistics, Brad continued. 'Jason your Cathay flight leaves at 6:00 p.m., and Tom, your Qantas flight at 6:30 p.m. Arrival times in Brisbane are 5:00 a.m. and 5:30 a.m. By then all hell should have broken loose here, so check on news stories as soon as you land. Jason, I suggest you arrange a secure pickup for the pair of you and that you go straight to your contact at the authorities.'

'Roger that.' Jason gave a thumbs up.

Adam reminded Jackson of Russell, the one who had kept him company while he waited for his flight in London. Same physique, and equally as talkative. Thoughts of London saddened him deeply. *Poor Ros. She didn't deserve to die in such a brutal manner.* Thinking about Ros again made him wonder what could have been. His thoughts quickly turned to anger and determination to expose the criminals who had overseen these recent heinous events.

Chapter 98

Marilyn Turner called Murray Jensen. He was feeling a little tired and had lost track of time. He gathered his thoughts and saw that it was 6:00 p.m. in Hong Kong, which was 10:00 a.m. London time. He'd been awake most of the night, and the lack of sleep was starting to take its toll.

'It's 6:00 p.m. here, Murray, and there is no sign of Jackson yet,' Marilyn began. 'That's a little odd, don't you think? He's been gone since before midday, and the sun is not far off setting.'

'I agree. You would have thought he might have returned to his room by now,' said Jensen, making his mind up as he spoke. 'Do it carefully, but I want you to break into his room and check for anything unusual. I still haven't heard from Andrew Wong, and am starting to have real concerns for his safety. Make sure the room is empty first, and be careful.'

'Will do. I'll call you shortly.'

Marilyn headed into the foyer of the hotel. She had anticipated such a request from Jensen and so had already befriended – and bribed – a member of the hotel staff. It was so easy, she thought, as she arranged access to level 48, where she'd discovered Jackson's room was. It would have been much more challenging to do this in London, but then the levels of security and CCTV surveillance in London were far more extensive than in most other first-world major cities.

On first entering the room, Marilyn thought everything looked normal. She carefully looked in the cupboards and the bathroom, and as

214

she started to leave, she noticed something. She returned to the bathroom and had a good look at the toiletries. Everything looked normal on first glance. On closer examination, however, she noticed that everything was new and unused, and, more significantly, every single item had been purchased in Hong Kong.

Marilyn returned to the room and opened the cupboards and clothes drawers. Same thing. All local apparel. *Where is his suitcase?* she wondered, and then it dawned on her. *He's not staying here anymore.* The room has been cleansed. *Clever.* No wonder she hadn't seen them return. They weren't going to.

*

Marilyn was careful to leave everything as she'd found it. She removed her gloves after she had calmly exited the room and then made her way back to reception. Once across the road, she called Murray Jensen.

'They're gone.'

'What do you mean gone?' *How could that be?* Murray fumed to himself.

Marilyn described what she'd discovered. 'It was very professionally done. I almost missed it myself.'

We'll never find them now, Jensen despaired to himself, and then said out loud, 'Go back to the office. Get some help and start a search of all of the five-star hotels. Look for Jackson and his investigator Jason Jones. If they're not at the five-star hotels, try the four-star ones. Report to me once you've done that, and, of course, earlier if you get any hits.'

'On to it,' Marilyn responded.

Murray ended the call and sat for a moment, analysing everything that had occurred since George Kim had called him earlier that day. Was it still the same day? Yes, but a very long one so far.

'Fuck,' Murray said out loud. The airport. They could have decided to leave Hong Kong altogether. This was getting away from him. He would lean on his contacts in the airline industry to see if they could track down any recent bookings for Jackson or Jones.

Chapter 99

Adam called Brad Charters from the Uber he and Jacqui had caught shortly after the last of the two flights to Australia had departed. 'Both safely in the air, boss. Where to now?'

'Good job, you two. Return to base for now and remain on call. Brett and I will take it from here. Bing is taking a time-out for a few hours. I don't expect I will need either of you, but the next phase is a dangerous one, so stay on standby.'

'Roger that.' Adam signed off.

Brett dropped Brad off near the head office for the Hong Kong Police Force, just around the corner from Pacific Place on Hong Kong Island. Brett was to remain in the vicinity on standby.

Brad had already made contact with his longstanding friend in the force, Deputy Commissioner Jeff Wu, who had agreed to stay in the office to meet with Brad.

'Brad. It's been some time since we last met.' Jeff began formally after Brad had been escorted to his office. 'To what do I owe this unexpected pleasure, and what's so important it couldn't have waited until tomorrow?'

Jeff was a career police officer with almost three decades experience in Hong Kong. Now in his late forties, he was as passionate now as he had been as a cadet about tracking down and incarcerating perpetrators of crime.

'Jeff. Nice to see you too.' Brad returned Jeff's grin. 'Are we safe in this room to chat freely?'

'Of course. Why wouldn't we be?' Jeff inclined his head a little.

Brad produced the USB Jackson had given him. 'Can I talk you through what's on this?' Before he gave the USB to Jeff, Brad repeated to Jeff much of what Tom Jackson and Jason Jones had told him earlier at the safe house.

The deputy commissioner remained silent throughout the recital. His eyes widened as parts of the story unfolded, and particularly when the connection was made to James Yeo's death earlier this afternoon. Jeff Wu had known Yeo quite well. They had been at school together, and hearing the story of what James may have become involved with both saddened and angered him.

Jeff took the USB and inserted it into the side of his computer. He opened the files it contained one by one. As he opened each file, Brad, who was also now looking at the computer screen that Jeff had partially turned in his direction, provided further details, as best he could, about the source of each of the documents and how they fitted in.

The commissioner spent some time reading James Yeo's statement. He read it a second time before looking up from his screen. Brad had been with him for over an hour.

'We need to be very careful with this.' Jeff Wu was deep in thought. 'I have been waiting for a breakthrough on this for many years. You probably don't know it but I went to school with James Yeo, and it saddens me to see the events that led to his suicide earlier today.'

Jeff and Brad talked for another fifteen minutes, before Jeff decided that he must assemble his special task force immediately. It was imperative that he moved swiftly so he could rely on the element of surprise. He knew from bitter experience that key players would quickly disappear once they became aware of the existence of this information.

Chapter 100

Murray Jensen had an extensive global network, and it wasn't long before he had confirmation that Jackson and Jones had departed from Hong Kong, heading for Brisbane, Australia. He was a little confused that they were on two separate flights. But that could simply be the result of separate travel arrangements at the outset, which made sense. On the other hand, it could be intentional to ensure that duplicates of the incriminating information he was now almost certain they must have were kept separate.

He called Marilyn to tell her the news, and to ask her to stand down. He was completely unaware that another set of the incriminating information had already been delivered to the Hong Kong Police Force.

His next call was to Sarina George in Brisbane. Sarina had been out of the loop for over a week, and a lot had happened in that time. Jensen quickly told her only what she needed to know. 'Be at the Brisbane International Airport by 5:00 a.m. tomorrow to meet both flights. I'll get instructions from the client and if I think you need extra muscle, I'll arrange it. As soon as I know more, I'll tell you.' He ended the call.

Jensen then called George Kim. 'Jackson and Jones have already left Hong Kong. They get back to Brisbane early tomorrow morning. I've already tasked one of my best assets to meet them on arrival and have plenty of time to assemble a support team, depending on what you want me to do.'

*

218

George Kim couldn't believe he was hearing this. 'You've never let me down before, Murray.'

'And I won't this time either, George.' Murray had faith in his operatives.

'Then make sure you grab them on arrival, and get back whatever James Yeo gave them. Don't dispense with either of them until we make sure they haven't passed the information on to anyone else.'

George was almost yelling. He was starting to panic, and was not thinking clearly. Even if the information had not been passed on, the execution of a prominent lawyer, together with a seasoned investigator who had been working for the lawyer, would attract more attention than he wanted to think about. He didn't care. He could always disappear if he had to. George Kim knew the game he was playing was a dangerous one, and he had long ago made contingency plans to disappear without trace on a moment's notice.

*

Murray Jensen was thinking that this was getting out of hand. But he didn't care either, so long as he was paid. He was certain the actions of his operatives could never be traced back to him. They were too careful, and so was he.

Chapter 101

Deputy Commissioner Jeff Wu had long suspected the existence of an illegal casino operating on Hong Kong Island. Each time he'd thought he had a lead or an information source, it mysteriously disappeared or dried up. He knew there must be a number of people on the force and in other governmental authorities who were on the payroll of the operators.

He had carefully selected the members of his special task force and ensured that at any point in time at least half of the members were on standby for deployment within the hour.

Jeff had assembled his team and raided the illegal casino within an hour of Brad's departure from his office. They had not been expecting it, and his team had been able to apprehend a significant number of casino staff, including many from middle management. His team had taken down the names of the patrons in attendance at the time of the raid, and they had been allowed to leave. They would be interviewed later, as needed.

It was imperative to the deputy commissioner that he locate and capture George Kim, who had been identified in the information Brad Charters had made available to him. He owed it to his friend James Yeo to capture Kim, and any as yet unidentified other members of the syndicate, and to shut this operation down once and for all.

Jeff Wu knew that it would have been unusual for George Kim to have been at the casino. He had already sent part of his team to Kim's private address to apprehend him, but he had not been there either.

News of the raid would spread like wildfire, so the deputy commissioner decided to go public with some of the details. That way he could release a photo of George Kim together with a statement that the police were searching for Mr Kim as they thought he could assist them with their investigations.

Chapter 102

Murray Jensen did not recognise the number that flashed up on his secure phone, so said nothing when he answered it.

'Murray Jensen, I believe,' said the caller with a sophisticated accent that was part British and part Chinese.

'Who wants to know?' Murray's senses were on full alert. This number was only given to well-known clients.

'Let's just say I am one of George Kim's colleagues. You may call me Adrian.'

'You could be anyone. How do I know you are who you say you are.' Murray was being deliberately evasive.

Adrian understood Jensen's concern, and proceeded to tell him in some detail what he knew about George Kim's interaction with him over the last fortnight.

'Thanks, Adrian. Can't be too sure in my game. How can I assist you?'

'One of our valuable operations in Hong Kong has been raided and shut down. It's not the end of the world, but it will hurt us a little. If it hasn't hit the international news feeds yet, it will shortly.'

Jensen was searching for the story as Adrian continued.

'You will see that the authorities are searching for George Kim, and so are we. The outcomes of George's recent activities have been, shall we say, somewhat disappointing, and we would like to talk to him before the authorities do. We're working on that. In the meantime, I thought I would call you to see what George's latest instructions were to you.'

Murray told Adrian of Kim's latest instructions to apprehend Jackson and Jones upon their arrival in Brisbane. He explained that he hadn't yet done so, but was about to organise an appropriate team to carry out George's instructions.

Adrian spoke in his businesslike tone. 'I would like you to please cease all operations on this file. George Kim will not be giving you any further instructions, and if he does, please ignore them and report to me.'

Murray Jensen wanted to interrupt, but thought better of it. He suspected that Adrian was a senior member of the powerful syndicate George Kim represented and did not wish to be on the wrong side of him.

Adrian continued. 'You have been paid twice the amount George Kim owed you for your excellent work, but I want that to be the end of it. Cease all operations, tie up any loose ends and close your file.'

While Adrian had been talking, Jensen had checked his bank account and confirmed that a double fee had been deposited a short while ago. 'I completely understand and will action your request immediately.'

'I knew you would.' Adrian signed off.

Chapter 103

Murray Jensen reflected on the call with 'Adrian' for some time. He was considering if there were any loose ends that he may have to tie up, and decided that there weren't any, except for his recent instruction to Sarina George.

It didn't sound like Mr Kim would be in any position to report on Murray's team's recent performance. His worst by far, he thought. He hoped Andrew Wong resurfaced so he could debrief him on recent events. If he didn't, Jensen would make sure his family was looked after, anonymously.

All that remained was to call Sarina and have her stand down permanently, at least in respect to this file.

He dialled her number. 'Sarina, my instructions on this file are cancelled. You are to stand down permanently. My full fee has been paid, and so will you be shortly. I will add a small bonus to reflect my appreciation for your good work on this.'

'Got it. It's been fun. Until next time then.' Sarina sounded disappointed but would know better than to protest. Murray Jensen was not someone to be taken lightly.

Chapter 104

George Kim had seen news of the raids on the casino and his own home. The news banner had appeared on his smart phone. As he made arrangements to implement his contingency plans, he reflected that it had been pure luck he had been neither at home nor at the casino at the time of the raids.

He knew he would be blamed by his other syndicate members for failing to protect one of their significant operations. The ramifications of an interrogation were unthinkable.

George had thought the plan to launder the money via the HK Investments deal had been a brilliant one. What had gone wrong? Tom Jackson was what went wrong. He cursed silently to himself as he thought about the role Jackson had played in his undoing. He had not come across anyone before who could not be influenced either by the threat of physical danger or the promise of money.

He consoled himself with the knowledge that he had sufficient funds and plans in place to disappear forever if need be. He also had plenty of time to reflect on his mistakes, and to consider whether revenge was warranted, or even possible.

Kim thought momentarily about alerting Richard Black to the situation, but quickly dismissed it. Richard could look after himself. In any event, the Pacific deal was as much Richard's idea as his, wasn't it?

Chapter 105

Day 16 (Tuesday)

Jones' flight landed first in Brisbane. As soon as he was permitted to do so, he activated his mobile phone and scanned the news alerts for Hong Kong.

It was the lead story. Silently he praised Brad Charters and his team.

He clicked on the link to the story headed, 'Illegal Casino on Hong Kong Island Raided and Shut Down. Many arrests have been made and police say more are expected.' The story went on to say that the police were actively searching for George Kim, who was thought to be a senior figure in the criminal organisation operating the casino.

Jones had a grin from ear to ear, and he mentally high-fived himself. He couldn't wait to tell Jackson.

First things first, he reminded himself. As soon as he entered the terminal, he found a quiet corner and called his contact in the state police, Inspector Joel Franklin. He knew it was early but also knew that Joel would take the call. The inspector knew Jason to be a serious operator who would not arbitrarily waste his time.

'G'day, Joel. Sorry to call so early, mate, but I have some real serious shit to discuss with you.'

'Jason. Great to hear from you. Go ahead.' Franklin had correctly guessed that Jason was in urgent need of his assistance.

As efficiently as he could, Jason took Inspector Franklin through the events of the last two weeks. The inspector asked a few brief questions throughout Jason's recital, and made a few comments such as, 'I have met Tom Jackson. Good operator.' And, 'I saw the news feed on James Yeo yesterday.'

By the time Jones had finished, Inspector Franklin had also read the news story on the Hong Kong casino raid. 'Extraordinary stuff, Jason. I'm not sure why you didn't involve me before now. We can chat about that later. These people are serious players. I'll send a protective unit to pick you and Jackson up from the airport. In the meantime, I'll assign someone at the airport to keep you safe.'

'Thanks heaps, mate. I knew you'd be the right fella to lay this on. I reckon you ought to nab Richard Black ASAP. Tom has thought for some time that Black is up to his eyeballs in this shit. The stuff we have from James Yeo proves it. He'll bolt as soon as he gets wind of all this, if he hasn't already.'

'Agreed, and onto it now. See you in the office in an hour or so. I'll call when we have Black.'

Jones was pleased with himself. Sure, he had a business to run, and he knew he would be well paid for this. Ridding the world of mega arseholes was just an added bonus.

Chapter 106

Richard Black had seen the disturbing news of James Yeo's suicide. Like George Kim, he now strongly suspected that Yeo must have provided Tom Jackson with incriminating evidence, once Jackson had confronted him with his own information. No doubt that's why Jackson had been accompanied by Jason Jones in the meeting. Maybe James Yeo had been able to piece together more than Richard had given him credit for.

Richard had tried on numerous occasions since seeing the news alert to make contact with George Kim. Each time, George's phone had diverted immediately to voice message. Either Kim was constantly on the phone, which was possible, or he had switched it to 'do not disturb' mode. The prospect of the second alternative troubled Richard.

He'd had a restless night and awoke early. Kim had not returned any of his calls, and his attempts to contact any other syndicate members had also been unsuccessful.

Perhaps it's time to disappear for a while, Richard thought. He had not been involved with the syndicate for as long as George Kim, and so had not yet seen fit to make the contingency plans that Kim had already activated. As he started to turn his mind to how he would go about quietly slipping away for a while, he heard the screech of tyres outside the front of his house. He peered through the curtains just in time to see a team of heavily armed state police charging at his front door. 'Police, open up,' they bellowed as the front door exploded from its hinges.

'On the floor now!' the lead officer yelled. His weapon was levelled at Richard's head.

In complete shock, Richard fell to his knees. Multiple strong hands forced him to lie face down on the floor. His arms were wrenched behind his back and his wrists handcuffed.

'What on earth is going on, Richard?' It was his wife Glenda, still half asleep. Her hand flew to her open mouth as she took in the scene in her lounge room.

'Sit down over there, ma'am,' said one of the officers. 'And don't move. We are arresting your husband in connection with an international criminal money laundering conspiracy and at least two suspected homicides.'

Glenda was in shock and unable to speak. She glared at her husband. Richard returned her gaze with a look of genuine sympathy and concern. *She had no idea, did she?* he thought. *You played the game well, Richard,* he congratulated himself. *Until now that is.* As he was half dragged and half carried to the waiting police van, he wondered why George Kim hadn't called to alert him.

Chapter 107

Jones was waiting for Jackson in the baggage collection hall. He was accompanied by two uniformed state police.

'Holy shit, Tom, have you seen the news?'

'Sure have. How good are Brad and his team?' Jackson was pleased, but still a little on edge. 'What's the local situation?'

'All sorted, mate. I've been on to that copper mate of mine, Inspector Joel Franklin. His team should have Richard Black by now, unless of course he's done a runner like George Kim. I expect to hear either way soon. In the meantime, he's assigned these two fine officers here to hold our hands until his protective unit arrives to take us to his office in the city.'

With the assistance of the state police, they cleared customs and exited by a side security door. This served to keep them away from prying eyes, and avoid any unnecessary enquiries.

*

Sarina George had been waiting with the crowd lined up to welcome home loved ones and colleagues. She was not sure why she had gone to the airport as originally planned, notwithstanding Murray Jensen's direction to cease all action on this file. Maybe it was purely curiosity, or just plain stubbornness. She had enjoyed her brief in this and had wished she'd been more in the loop. It had been more than half an hour since Jackson's flight had landed, and over an hour since Jones' had, with no sign of either of them. Despondently, she headed for the exit. As she did so, she witnessed a special operations team of police escorting the men she'd been scoping out to a waiting van. *Whoa,* she thought. *I get it now. I'm outta here.*

Chapter 108

The inside of the police van was surprisingly comfortable.

Jones' phone rang. 'Jones, here. Yes, mate. Friggin' good news. Yeah, the stuff we'll bring to you shortly will more than back up what I told you on the phone. Thanks, mate. I trust you too.'

Jason high-fived Tom, who looked at him with eager anticipation. 'Well?'

'They got the fucker before he bolted. Not sure why that bastard Richard Black was still around, but they have already arrested him. My guess is that he had probably seen the story on James Yeo, but that he hadn't yet picked up on the casino raid. That prick George Kim probably didn't call Black to alert him. Too busy trying to save his own skin, I reckon. I was just assuring my mate Franklin that the information we have is rock solid.' Jason sat back in his seat and allowed himself to relax for the first time in a while. He noticed Tom do the same.

Jackson sat up and looked at his watch. It was 7:30 a.m. 'I must ring Max and explain. He'll be wondering about the information I sent him, and is no doubt concerned for my wellbeing.'

He dialled Max's number. 'Hey Max. Early-ish I know, sorry, but I wanted to let you know that Jason and I have returned safely from Hong Kong.'

'Holy crap, Tom. You guys sure knocked it out of the park. That information you sent me was gold. I've seen the news on James Yeo and the casino raid. I assume you also have the local side sorted?'

'I'll tell you more when I come into the office tomorrow. You won't believe what we've been through. More cloak and dagger stuff in a couple of days than you and I have seen in a lifetime. Just on our way to the state police now. They've already taken Richard Black into custody. All okay in the office?'

'Glad you guys are safe. As for the office, what can I say. Same shit, different depth.' Max laughed infectiously.

'You're the IT expert, Max. Can you lock the files I sent you in an electronic vault, accessible by only you and me? I'm sure we won't need any of it, but you know I like to have contingency plans in place.' Jackson didn't seriously think he would need to rely on Max's copies of the information, but it was better to be safe than sorry.

'Done. Rest up and we'll chat tomorrow.'

Chapter 109

The trip into the city did not take very long. The van passed the state police building's secure checkpoint and descended into the basement car park.

Inspector Joel Franklin was waiting for them as they exited the lift on the top level of the building. After Jason made the introductions, the inspector's PA took a coffee order from everyone. Tom was relieved to hand over the original documents he'd been clutching almost continuously since he'd left James Yeo's office. He found it hard to believe that had been less than twenty-four hours ago.

Jackson provided a comprehensive recap of all that had transpired since the first Pacific board meeting a little over two weeks ago. Inspector Franklin and Jones were transfixed as Tom described an unbelievable two-week period. Jackson could hardly believe the incredible story himself. It all seemed surreal, but the three deaths made it real, particularly the first two. *Poor Ros*, he thought again to himself for the umpteenth time.

Franklin had listened intently to the lawyer without comment. He had heard most of the key parts from Jones, and was pleased to have verbal corroboration from Jackson, whose reputation he knew to be tough yet fair. He took his time to thumb through the original documents Tom had provided, starting with James Yeo's statement. Finally he looked up at them and shook his head slowly.

'I don't know whether to berate you, or offer you a job, Jason. This is dangerous stuff. I can't understand why you didn't involve the police much earlier in the process.'

'Simple, mate. Couldn't prove a bloody thing. The bad guys were that good. Also, we weren't too sure who we could trust.' Jason sounded sincere.

'You must tell me one day which resources you had access to in Hong Kong. We sure could learn a thing or two from them,' the inspector said with genuine admiration.

Jones tapped the side of his nose 'Mum's the word, sorry. You know we special investigators like to keep some of the secret squirrel shit to ourselves.'

'I'll have my team take you to your home, Tom, and, just to be sure, we'll keep a watch over you for the next few days.'

'Thanks, Joel,' Jackson said as he shook his hand. Jason gave Franklin a huge bear hug. The inspector had known Jones for years, but sometimes he forgot just how different the man was.

Jones had decided to stay in a hotel Brisbane CBD for a few more days just to be available if he was needed for anything.

Chapter 110

DAY 17 (Wednesday)

Jackson slept soundly, and didn't wake until well after his usual time. He then made contact with Kevin Lightfoot, Acting Chair of the Pacific Property Board. 'Kevin. Tom Jackson here.'

'Tom, no need to ask you how your trip to Hong Kong was. I've already heard and read about the outcomes. Extraordinary stuff. I still can't believe that Richard Black has been arrested. He was a difficult bastard I know, but part of an international crime syndicate? Really?'

'You better believe it,' Jackson said. 'I can't and don't need to tell you everything, but I should tell you and the board what I'm able to. Would you please convene a board meeting for today or tomorrow?'

'Absolutely. Other board members have been on to me, and we are all keen to know where we stand. Obviously the deal is off, but an explanation would be helpful, thanks Tom. I'm sure they'll be available for a meeting later today. I'll get back to you with a time, unless you have a preference. I'll also have the chief operating officer, Margaret Addison, attend the meeting. After Richard's arrest yesterday, she is now acting CEO. Marg is a good operator, who will probably be confirmed as Pacific's next CEO. One thing at a time, however.'

'Cheers, Kevin. I'll wait till I hear from you. I should be in the office mid to late morning, but please call my mobile in case I'm out and about. A meeting any time after lunch would suit, thanks.'

Chapter 111

Jackson knew his police protective unit would take care of any security issues. He wasn't expecting that there would be anything to worry about, but just to be sure he kept a sharp eye out for that silver AMG Mercedes and anything else unusual.

He arrived at work without incident and, as he headed for Max Grenfell's office, he literally bumped into Roger Everingham, who had been skulking about the corridors. *Does he ever do any work?*

'Tom. Back so soon? Did you have anything to do with what's been happening in Hong Kong?' He always had a friendly tone, but he rarely meant it. His inane question suggested to Jackson that Roger had once again engaged his mouth before his brain.

Everingham said he'd seen the disturbing news about James Yeo, and Tom thought he looked very concerned.

He had good cause for concern, thought Tom, glaring at Everingham. *This shithead is partly to blame for the deaths of Ros Green and Ian Fox, and will most definitely pay for it.* Yeo had carefully documented his arrangement with Everingham and had recorded all information received.

Jackson wasn't in the mood for Roger, so he simply shook his head in mild disgust and continued walking. *There will be a more appropriate opportunity very soon to expose your role and ensure you suffer the consequences of your disgraceful actions, you prick.*

Max Grenfell was waiting for him. He shook hands vigorously with Tom and leaned in for a half-man hug and slap on the back. 'Great job, mate. Ridiculously dangerous, but well executed. Do you think it's over?'

'Yes,' Jackson said confidently. 'Got time now for a download?'

'Of course.'

Jackson talked Max through the menacing events that had unfolded in Hong Kong. Max sat spellbound and said nothing until Jackson had finished.

'You're a very smart man, Tom. Risky stuff, but the stakes were incredibly high, and you were smart enough to engage the right people to assist. I get why you did it. It wasn't just about the deal. Your decency would not have allowed you to stop after the unfortunate events that took place in London. You must be very relieved that you're alive . For what it's worth, I agree with your conclusion that it's over. Glad to have you back in one piece, man.'

Max moved towards Jackson as if he was planning another man hug, but to Tom's relief shook his hand vigorously instead. 'You're a good man, mate. By the way, I saw you chatting to that scumbag Everingham before you came into my office. Anything of significance?'

'Let's just say I felt like I needed a bath after I bumped into him. Hopefully that will be one of the last times.'

Max stood motionless, his eyebrows raised in anticipation. 'What do you mean by that?'

'Fortunately for us, and for the professional world at large, James Yeo faithfully recorded every detail of Everingham's involvement. I did not include that information in the package I sent you simply because I wanted to see the look on your face when you read the details.' Tom handed over Yeo's file notes on his conversations with Everingham, as well as a ledger setting out details of payments made to the corrupt bastard.

Grenfell's eyes widened as he read the information. 'Everingham will certainly be expelled from the partnership, and may even lose his practising certificate. How do you plan on dealing with this explosive information?'

Tom told Max what he planned to do about Everingham in the lead up to the next partner's meeting on Thursday and asked him to keep the details to himself.

'I never tell anyone anything you tell me, unless you expressly authorise it.'

Tom knew that to be absolutely true. 'Thanks for your help on this, Max. You're a good friend and colleague. I need to now get ready for a board meeting at Pacific Property shortly after lunch.'

'That should be interesting. Good luck.' Max sat down at his desk and picked up the phone to make a call. He had a lot happening today, but had held off doing much until he'd caught up with Jackson.

Chapter 112

Kevin Lightfoot had emailed Jackson to confirm the Pacific board meeting at 2:30 p.m., and Tom had acknowledged the email and confirmed the time.

He then called Jennifer Armitage. 'Jennifer, how are you? I understand Ian's funeral was held on Monday. I'm so sorry for your loss.'

Jennifer inhaled audibly before she spoke. 'Thank you, Tom. I'm doing okay, all things considered.'

'We have a Pacific board meeting at 2:30 p.m., and I wanted to meet with you beforehand to tell you in detail what's happened since we spoke last Thursday. Do you have time?' Jackson felt that he owed Jennifer a more complete description of what took place than the one he planned to tell the board. He thought it would give her a little more closure to realise that justice would be served, and that Ian had played a key role in discovering the truth.

'Sure, Tom. I haven't been able to concentrate much since Ian's funeral. Why don't you come over to my office now if that suits?'

'See you in about twenty minutes.' Jackson wanted to brief his team on the status of the deal, although he was certain they would already know it would not be proceeding, not with this financier anyway.

Chapter 113

Jennifer Armitage gave Tom a friendly embrace as soon as they were alone in a meeting room at her office. 'Thank you for setting this right. It's good to know that Ian did not die in vain. I hope the information I gave you was of some assistance.'

'More than that, Jennifer.' Jackson sat down as she did. 'Without the information from Ian's investigators, I suspect we would still not have been able to expose the fraud. It was your courage in seeing Ian's investigations continued that provided the missing link.

'The casino ownership connection allowed Jason Jones and I to confront James Yeo. Fortunately for all of us, he turned out to have a conscience and, when confronted with the truth, did the right thing.' Tom spent some time telling Jennifer everything that took place in Hong Kong.

'I can't believe you took such a personal risk to become so involved in this.' Jennifer was genuinely shocked at the description of what he had been through.

'I felt I owed it to Ian and Ros to do the best I could. There were never any guarantees of course, and at times I wasn't quite sure what I had gotten myself into. The deal didn't seem quite right from the outset, so I knew the deeper we dug, the more chance my investigator and I had of seeing through the falsehoods.' Tom could see that Jennifer was exhausted from her personal ordeal.

'Ironic, isn't it, that it all unravelled for the criminals in another country on the day we buried poor Ian?' Jennifer was gazing out the window, deep in thought.

Tom gently put his hand on Jennifer's shoulder to comfort her. 'Small consolation I'm sure, but Ian's death will not have been for nothing. The authorities are casting a wide net and will no doubt see that as many of these scoundrels as possible are brought to justice.'

She seemed grateful for his sympathetic gesture and words, and smiled at him.

'I should head back to the office to tidy up a few things ahead of our meeting this afternoon. Will you be okay?'

'Of course, Tom. Thank you for your concerns and for coming to see me to explain everything. See you at the board meeting this afternoon.' Jennifer looked to have perked up a little, likely due to the sense of closure she could now start to feel.

Chapter 114

Kevin Lightfoot formally opened the meeting. 'Thank you all for attending. I declare the board meeting open and invite Tom Jackson to update us on recent events relating to the Pacific Property deal with HK Investments.'

Jackson sat in the same chair he had been in a little over two weeks ago. It was almost too much for him to contemplate what had transpired in the intervening period. He looked around the table at Kevin Lightfoot, Shaun Ingram, Jennifer Armitage, Margaret Addison (the new acting CEO) and Peter Tomlinson. With the exception of Tomlinson, each wore a look of almost sad resignation. Peter looked as if he was ready for an argument.

'Point of order, Mr Chairman. May I speak briefly first?' It was Tomlinson.

As if Kevin had been expecting this, he nodded for Peter to continue.

'When I spoke to you last Friday, Tom, you assured me that your trip to Hong Kong had nothing to do with the HK Investments deal.' Peter's tone was such that everyone around the table tensed a little.

Tom wondered where this was headed, but said nothing. He had noticed that Kevin Lightfoot did not look too concerned.

Peter continued. 'I take it that when we spoke you were still undecided whether or not to trust me?'

Jackson was about to say something, but Peter continued on before he could. 'I get it, Tom.' Peter's tone softened. 'On behalf of the board,

I would like to sincerely thank you for the significant role you have played in uncovering the awful truths that you had clearly suspected much earlier than any of us. We owe you a debt of gratitude. I know it won't truly compensate you for what you've been through, but I move that Tom's legal fee be paid in full, and the success-fee component also be paid as if the deal had proceeded.'

Without being asked by the chair to do so, each of the directors raised their hand in unanimous support for the motion.

Jackson was gobsmacked. He hadn't expected this. 'Thanks, Peter, and directors. I'm very grateful.' Tom had never been driven by money, and firmly believed that good work would always produce appropriate rewards. That said, he was under constant pressure to satisfy the backroom numbers people within the firm.

'We would also like you to work with us on finding alternative sources of finance for our project,' Margaret Addison chimed in. 'It's a great project, and we are still keen for it to proceed, although we recognise we'll need to be realistic about appropriate levels of return.'

Kevin Lightfoot invited Jackson to continue. 'With that out of the way, Tom, please proceed with your report on the status of the project.'

'I appreciate the continuing brief on the project, and will tap into my network to see which financiers may be interested in syndicating a loan for it.' Tom spent the next thirty minutes giving a factual version of events since the last board meeting a little under two weeks ago. No one said anything. While all of the directors knew many of the facts, most were quietly in awe to hear Tom describe the events as they had unfolded. Out of respect for Jennifer, he kept his comments on Ian Fox's role to a minimum, but at the same time left them with no doubt that his role had been a pivotal one.

'Thanks, Tom.' Kevin was keen to wrap the meeting up. 'There's one more item on the agenda. Ros Green's family have been in contact with us about a memorial service for her. It is to be held on Friday at 11 a.m. in St Stephens Cathedral in the city. We are all invited. Her remains were cremated in a private service in London last week, and her ashes will be interred following Friday's memorial service.' All at the meeting confirmed they would attend on Friday, and they parted company.

244

Chapter 115

Jackson's feelings were mixed as he headed back to the offices of Ridgeway Mason. He felt satisfied in a professional sense and reflected that just like many times in the past, albeit without the immense personal risk he had faced on this occasion, he had been able to establish the complete absence of bona fides in this transaction. It never ceased to amaze him how much illegal money was coursing through the financial veins of the world's economy, looking for a legitimate home, nor how sophisticated the attempts to achieve that were becoming.

In a personal sense, however, he regretted that he had put Ros at risk, and he was still having trouble coming to terms with the deaths of two completely innocent people, especially hers. That didn't mean he was at peace with the death of James Yeo. Sure, James had made his own bed, but he was also the victim of criminal manipulation.

Tom called a team meeting to tell them the good news that the firm's engagement had been extended to assisting Pacific in sourcing legitimate funding for the deal. They were also delighted to hear that Pacific had agreed to pay not only the full fee for the deal, but the success-fee component as if the deal had proceeded. Jackson looked forward to reporting this at tomorrow night's partners' meeting.

One more thing to do before I head home. He dialled Jason Jones' number. 'Sleep okay last night?'

'Like a friggin' baby, mate. You?'

'I actually slept in, which is unusual for me. Must have needed it.'

'Good stuff. How'd the Pacific board meeting go?'

'I met separately with Jennifer first to tell her everything. She took comfort from the knowledge that Ian Fox's information was vital to exposing the fraud, and I think she'll be able to find some sort of closure.'

'Nice one, mate,' said Jones.

'The board meeting itself was interesting. I think it was a set-up between the acting chairman, Kevin Lightfoot, and Peter Tomlinson, but at the outset it looked as if Peter wanted to tear strips off me. He then moved a motion of thanks, and the board voted unanimously to pay my full fee, including the success-fee component, as if the deal had proceeded to conclusion. Your fee and add-on costs will be paid in full, and I plan to share part of my success fee of $500,000 with you. I'm proposing to give you twenty-five per cent of it, $125,000. I will, of course need the consent of my partners, but expect that will be forthcoming at tomorrow night's partners' meeting.'

'Holy shit, mate. Had to pick myself up off the floor. Are you sure?' Jones sounded genuinely surprised. 'No one has ever done that for me before.'

'Absolutely.' Jackson was smiling to himself. He liked this man. 'The memorial service for Ros Green is at St Stephens Cathedral in the city on Friday morning at 11a.m. Will you be attending?'

'I'll be there, mate. See you then.' Jones signed off.

Chapter 116

That was enough for today, Jackson decided. As he headed home, he saw the police protective unit take its position behind his car. He wondered how long this would be necessary. For now he was glad to have such visible protection.

Over the course of the evening, Tom pondered the events of the last fortnight. *Life is so fragile, and we all tread such a fine line.* His thoughts returned again to what might have been with Ros, and sadness mixed with an overwhelming sense of anger consumed him for some time. Jackson knew that it was easy to recalibrate with the benefit of hindsight, but knew better than to dwell on matters beyond his control. He resolved to focus his attention on the one remaining thing he had a measure of control over: exacting revenge on Everingham.

Chapter 117

DAY 18 (Thursday)

Jackson arrived later, after avoiding the traffic again. He could get used to this, but his clients would never allow it of course. More often than not, his clients insisted that Jackson remained involved at the coal face. They respected that he had a great team, but he was sure their unanimous preference would be for him to simply clone himself. Some had actually said as much.

'G'day, Max. Sorry to drop in unannounced.'

'No problem, Tom. What's up?' Max Grenfell was always happy to make time available for Jackson. They had been through a lot together.

'I need to run something past you ahead of tonight's meeting.'

'I'm all ears, mate.'

Jackson ran through what he had in mind for the meeting.

'I like it. As I keep saying, you're a smart man, and I reckon that'll achieve the outcomes you want.'

'Thanks, Max. I'll let you get on with your work. I know how busy you are. See you at 5:00 p.m.'

Jackson left Max's office and headed for Frederick Anderson's. As the newly minted managing partner of the Brisbane office, Anderson usually made himself available to his fellow partners on short notice. Today was no different.

Anderson looked up from his desk as he saw Jackson at the door. 'Tom. Come in. Take a seat.'

248

Jackson dodged Anderson's expensive street bicycle on the way in. In his mid-fifties, Anderson was tall with a full head of distinguished grey hair. He cycled to and from work most days, resulting in a physique like a racing greyhound. Despite his at-times officious manner, Anderson had a kind disposition and was very skilled at allowing all sides of a discussion to be fully explored in any meeting he presided over.

Tom allowed himself to relax a little as he sat down opposite Anderson and looked him directly in the eye. 'I need to discuss a serious matter I plan to raise at tonight's meeting, and I thought it best not to put you on the spot without notice.'

He had Anderson's full attention, who leaned forward a little and nodded for Jackson to continue. Tom gave a brief update on recent critical events in case Anderson was not fully across them. It was clear that he was, but Tom wanted to be sure.

'What hasn't yet surfaced is this.' Tom handed him James Yeo's hand written note of his conversations with Roger Everingham and the ledgers showing payments made by Yeo to Everingham.

Jackson saw Anderson's mouth fall open as he immediately grasped the significance of the documents. Tom explained what he had in mind for the meeting and what he would like Frederick to do beforehand. Anderson readily gave his consent.

Chapter 118

Tom Jackson was always well prepared for the partners' meetings. Even though theoretically his fellow partners should have been at the very least good business colleagues, there was always someone who was pursuing a hidden agenda. There was also the hostile collective of six, as Max called them, headed by Everingham and Fletcher, who always seemed to be working contrary to the best interests of the advancement of the business. Jackson could never really understand that, but then he had learnt long ago that not everybody's behaviour was dictated by logic.

Fred Anderson called the meeting to order shortly after 5:15 p.m. Jackson had no idea why these meetings could not start at the appointed time. For some reason many lawyers, and partners in particular, were missing the punctuality gene.

Jackson saw that twenty out of the twenty-five partners in Ridgeway Mason's Brisbane office were present. A very good turnout, Jackson reflected. He noticed that Roger Everingham and Miles Fletcher were among those present, as were another three of their particular faction.

Fred then presented the firm's results for the preceding calendar month and the year to date, by practice group. The results were displayed both numerically and graphically on the large screen on the wall at the foot of the boardroom table. The screen was controlled from a computer operated by one of the faceless backroom numbers men who seemed to take delight in pointing out any shortfalls against budget.

'I'll run through the numbers for each group, and then will invite each group head to report,' Anderson continued.

He addressed Tom when it was his turn to report on the activities of his group. 'Tom, I know it's only been a few weeks since the last special partners' meeting, but I understand a lot's been happening in your patch. Your report should be interesting.'

'Thanks, Fred.' Jackson began. 'Before I report on the detail, there is something I need to address. You have no doubt all seen the press about the Pacific Property deal with HK Investments, and the events in London and Hong Kong.' All around the table were nodding. 'The source of the $750 million funds for the deal turned out to be the proceeds of an illegal casino operation in Hong Kong. Some serious criminal elements are involved, and, unfortunately, not all of them are likely to be brought to justice. In addition to the death of James Yeo that you have all no doubt heard about, two innocent people, Ros Green, the former chair of Pacific Property, and Ian Fox, the forensic accountant who was the partner of Jennifer Armitage, one of Pacific's directors, have been murdered.'

Tom stopped talking for a minute or two to let this information sink in. He knew that, while most would have heard of the deaths of Ros and Ian, only a very few would have known that their deaths were connected.

'Fortunately, James Yeo had a conscience. When Jason Jones and I confronted him with the truth, he produced a file from his safe that allowed us to prove to the authorities in both Hong Kong and here in Brisbane that a global criminal conspiracy to launder illegal moneys was in play.'

Jackson noticed that Roger Everingham and Miles Fletcher looked particularly uncomfortable. Roger was working to loosen his tie.

'It was very apparent to me from James Yeo's file that someone had been feeding him information about my role in this transaction and what my plans were from time to time. The release of that information would certainly have played a role in the death of at least Ros Green.'

Everingham was actually squirming in his seat, and beads or perspiration were beginning to form on Fletcher's forehead. *Got you, you bastards,* Jackson thought, savouring the moment before he continued.

'I plan to commission a forensic audit of my work and private email accounts, and also those of my PA, Samantha Brown. Samantha is the only one who has delegated authority to access my emails. The analysis will be done, and the results known, before the end of next week. Copies of the initial report will be made available to Fred, myself and our CEO in Sydney.'

Jackson did not wait for any verbal or other form of consent from those present to what he was proposing. It was not a matter for debate. He was merely informing them.

Roger Everingham and Miles Fletcher appeared to relax a little.

'There's one more important issue on this particular topic. With your permission, Fred, I'll continue.' Jackson looked to Andreson who nodded his assent, with a hard stony stare in Everingham's direction.

Jackson motioned for the operator to display James Yeo's documents on the large screen for all to see. It didn't take long for the reactions. They were varied – from speechlessness to loud vocal displays of righteous indignation. Everingham stood up as if to leave.

'Sit down, Roger.' Anderson commanded over the cacophony. The room fell silent as Anderson continued, his alert, piercing gaze leaving none in doubt that he had the floor. If it wasn't such a serious matter, Tom would have enjoyed the theatrics more.

'Tom has provided me with the originals of the documents you can all see on the screen. While not critical to the process, it's likely the results of the forensic audit process Tom has mentioned will supplement the damning evidence you see before you. I sent the information to our CEO and General Counsel in Sydney and discussed it with each just before this meeting. A Notice of Expulsion from the partnership will be prepared and delivered to you, Roger, tomorrow, and the matter will be referred to the Law Society.'

Everingham moved to speak but was neatly silenced by a sharp wave of Anderson's hand. 'You will have a chance to protest your innocence and put forward any mitigating circumstances during the formal expulsion process.' Anderson paused for effect. 'Are there any queries or comments on this?'

There were none.

Tom noticed that the bean counter had changed the screen to now display the financials for his team. A look from Anderson told him he should continue with his report.

'Moving on to my team's financials,' Jackson continued, glaring at Everingham as he left the room in shame, clutching his crumpled suit jacket and slowly shaking his head from side to side. 'In addition to the results displayed on the screen, I am pleased to report that the Pacific Property Board voted at its meeting yesterday to pay not only my total agreed fee of $1.5 million in the now-aborted deal with HK Investments, but also my success fee of $500,000 as if the deal had proceeded to conclusion. As you will hear shortly when I tell you what happened in London and Hong Kong, Jason Jones from JJ Investigations played an integral role in unravelling the conspiracy and, more importantly, in keeping me safe throughout the ordeal. I propose to pay twenty-five per cent of the success fee, an amount of $125,000, to Jones for the invaluable role he played. With Fred's consent I would like you all to hold your comments on my proposal until you hear what actually happened over the last couple of weeks.'

'Granted,' said Anderson, as if he were in a court room.

Jackson then calmly took them through the events of the last two-and-a-half weeks. It took almost half an hour. As with each other time he had done this, no one said a word. Max had heard it before but he too was gobsmacked by the events and just kept shaking his head in admiration at how well Tom had handled each situation.

'Obviously there is still further work to be done by the police, both here and in Hong Kong, but it is now well and truly under control. One final thing: The Pacific board has retained the firm to assist with assembling a syndicate of legitimate financiers for their Edward Street project, which they still wish to proceed with.'

Many of those around the table wanted to applaud Jackson, but their own feelings of insecurity prevented any of them from doing so.

'Well done, Tom. This will make the Brisbane office look good.' Anderson sounded as if he were entitled to take some of the credit. 'I am very strongly in favour of your suggested payment to JJ Investigations. Does anyone disagree?'

The room was silent. 'Good, then. It's approved. Tom, I will leave it to you to action this.' Frederick continued. 'As Tom's was the last report, I declare the meeting closed. Please stay for drinks.' It was a directive rather than a request. A directive that Tom and Max usually ignored, but not this time.

Chapter 119

Max followed Tom to his office, and shut the door. 'Great presentation, mate. Well done. Those pricks will be shitting themselves, particularly Everingham.'

They talked between themselves for another ten minutes or so about what the forensic investigation might reveal, before Max announced he was heading home. 'Thanks again for all your support,' Jackson said.

'De nada,' said Max. Tom knew that was Spanish for you're welcome, but wasn't sure why Max had reverted to another language.

Tom called Jason Jones before heading home, to tell him the good news about the bonus payment of $125,000. Jones was over the moon and moved to an outburst of profanity to express his gratitude. Jackson was pleased that he could share the success fee with Jones. He certainly deserved it. He would leave it to Jason to determine if he would share any with Brad Charter's team in Hong Kong. Pacific had separately agreed to pay Jason's and Brad's operational fees and costs, so Tom knew that neither was out of pocket. Nor should they be.

On the way home, he wondered what he would do if the forensic analysis of his email accounts confirmed his suspicions that Miles Fletcher was also involved. *Not my problem for now,* Jackson thought, as he reflected on the pleasure he'd derived in seeing Everingham out the door, literally. He was certain that the Notice of Expulsion from the partnership would not be successfully challenged, and he hoped the Law Society would permanently remove Everingham's right to practise law. The society may also refer the matter to the police to investigate whether Everingham could be charged with aiding and abetting criminal activity. While Everingham would certainly get was coming to him, it would not bring back Ros or Ian. Thinking of their senseless deaths made him boil with anger, and he gripped the steering wheel until his knuckles whitened.

Chapter 120

George Kim had managed to avoid the Hong Kong authorities. With the first leg of his journey to Central America complete, he sat in a restaurant somewhere in Southern China reflecting again on what had gone wrong. Tom Jackson was all he could think about. He wondered if he should disappear as planned, or if he should do something else. Kim was not one to readily accept defeat.

He called Murray Jensen. 'Murray, its George. I need you to do something for me.'

Jensen knew that he would not be doing whatever George asked him to, but knew he could better serve Adrian Low's interests if he heard what the man had to say. 'I'm not sure, George. There's a little too much heat at the moment, unless it's not connected with the James Yeo thing.'

Kim was not accustomed to having Murray question him. 'I have always paid you well, Murray.'

'Correct,' Jensen replied. But Adrian had recently paid him twice the amount George had promised.

'Then hear me out, please.'

Murray had not heard George Kim use the word please before, so was intrigued.

Kim continued. 'I'm in the process of disappearing, but wanted you to assist with setting things right for me. Tom Jackson has cost me dearly. I may never recover from this, and am resigned to the fact that I must start a new life.'

Jensen knew better than to ask George where he was or where he may be headed, but he wanted to draw him out a little further. 'What do you need?'

'I want Jackson terminated with extreme prejudice. There will be a bonus in it for you if you also take out Jason Jones.' George Kim was almost spitting his words into the phone.

'I'm not sure I can do that.' Murray was enjoying baiting the man. It was nice to not be on the receiving end for a change.

Kim was almost speechless. 'What are you talking about? I give the instructions, you do the work, and I pay. That's how it works. That's how it has always worked. Is it the money? Is that what this is about? Do you want to be paid more?'

Jensen could hear that George was desperate. 'No, it's not the money. On occasion, I choose to refuse instructions where I believe the risks outweigh the rewards. This is one of those occasions.'

'Fine. I'll do it myself,' George said determinedly, and he ended the call.

'Bingo,' Murray said to himself. He dialled Adrian's number immediately. 'Adrian, I've just heard from George Kim.'

'Did he say where he was?'

'No, but I know where he's headed.'

They discussed what Adrian required.

'Send me a recent photo of George Kim, and I'll head there myself with my best London operative, Charles Sanderson. I'll call you when it's done,' Murray said.

Jensen had decided on the run that the tasks set by Adrian were beyond Sarina's capabilities. He needed to be certain this was done properly.

He contacted Charles Sanderson and made arrangements to charter a jet. He wasn't sure where Kim was, but calculated that if he left soon, he could be in Brisbane by no later than very early Saturday morning, local time.

Chapter 121

DAY 19 (Friday)

Jackson had decided to work remotely on Friday. The primary focus was to attend the memorial service for Ros at St Stephens Cathedral.

He arrived early at the memorial service. Tom liked to be early for everything, but in particular for events such as these. He could then speak to each participant he knew, as they arrived.

St Stephens Cathedral was a magnificent building with lengthy and extensive refurbishment having only recently been completed. More than 200 people had decided to attend the service. The church was more than capable of comfortably accommodating that number.

Tom and Jason sat with Jennifer Armitage. Tom knew that Ros had been a wonderful person, but hadn't appreciated just how well loved she was. The eulogy was given by Ros's sister and there were two other tributes given by respected business people, as well as her ex-husband. They had only been recently divorced.

After the service was over and Tom had paid his respect to Ros's family, he chatted for a while with Jennifer and Jason in private.

'Are the coppers still watching over you, mate?' Jones asked.

'For now, yes. There is, however, now only one officer involved. There are still a few loose ends, but I'm not expecting all of them to be tied off. I understand the continued need for the protective unit is to be reviewed by your mate Inspector Joel Franklin early next week.'

'I have some good news,' Jennifer piped up. She had been silent for the entire service, no doubt reflecting on Ian's funeral earlier in the week. Her sudden comment surprised both of them.

'We're all in need of some good news, Jennifer. What is it?' enquired Tom.

'I'm pregnant with Ian's baby. His memory will live on through his child.' Jennifer looked both happy and sad.

Tom and Jason each took turns in congratulating her. *The cycle of life.* Tom was thinking of Mary again and how much he knew she would love to have a family. But the cut and thrust of their careers had made that impossible. He was genuinely happy for Jennifer.

Chapter 122

DAY 20 (Saturday)

Murray Jensen's flight touched down at 5 a.m. on the Saturday. Before they left London, and while refuelling at Dubai, he had been able to ascertain from his contacts which flights had arrived in Brisbane directly from China the day before, and which were due to arrive that morning.

He knew George Kim would be using an alias, but felt it was safe to assume that he had not yet left China at the time he'd spoken with Murray. That being the case, Kim had either arrived late yesterday, or would be arriving shortly. Rather than wait at the airport, Murray and Charles collected their hire car, booked under an alias, and headed for Jackson's home in Paddington.

They immediately saw the police protective unit across the road from Tom's house. They weren't surprised that he was still under protection, but were pleasantly surprised to see that it was only one officer.

'As soon as George Kim shows up, neutralise the bobby, Charles, but don't hurt him. I'll check out security at the rear of the house.'

'Got it, guv. You seem certain Kim will show up?'

He already had.

Chapter 123

Jackson was a light sleeper, and he heard an unusual sound at the rear downstairs door. Fortunately, he was security conscious. When he'd lived with Mary, they'd installed Crimsafe steel mesh on all window and door openings shortly after they had purchased the house, and every night before going to bed he checked that each door was locked.

Instead of opening the front door, Tom thought it best to call the officer. At his insistence he'd been provided with the direct mobile number of each officer on duty. There was no answer. He peered through the louvres in the front lounge room. He could see the police car across the road, but the officer appeared to be slumped forward.

Shit. He quickly decided to call Jason Jones first before dialling triple zero. 'Jason, sorry to wake you. Someone's trying to get in downstairs, and the policeman across the road looks to have been taken out.' Jackson was flexing his muscles as he spoke

'On my way. I'll call my copper Franklin on the way. Be there in around ten minutes. Sit tight, and grab a baseball bat or a knife, or something to protect yourself with.'

Who needs a baseball bat, Jackson thought, recalling his Krav Maga training as he silently descended the stairs. Then Tom heard a deep voice but it wasn't addressing him.

'George Kim, I presume?' Murray Jensen wrapped his strong arm around George's throat. 'What were you planning to do, George, shoot the locks off like they do in the movies?'

Tom burst out of his back door, knocking Jensen to the ground. He grabbed the man who he now knew to be George Kim and wrestled him to the ground with ease. As he jumped up, a swift kick behind Kim's left ear left him prone on the ground. Jackson reacted instinctively to new movement to his left. Jensen had quickly regained his feet and was moving in to attack. *This guy knows what he's doing,* thought Tom as he took up his defensive stance. As good as Jensen was, he was no match for Tom's extensive martial arts training. After a few quick encounters, Tom had bested Jensen and was thinking quickly how to convert his restraining hold on him into something more permanent when he detected further movement.

'Bobby's neutralised, guv,' another voice said. 'We need to move. I saw Jackson peering through the front window. Others will arrive.' Sanderson stopped mid-sentence as he took in the scene before him. Without another thought, his special forces instincts took over. He launched at Jackson and clocked him on the side of the head with the short, heavy fighting stick he'd just used on the police officer. Tom had had insufficient time to release Jensen and fend off Sanderson's attack. All he could do was turn his head slightly in an effort to deflect the severity of the blow that he knew was to come. Jackson heard the loud crack as the weapon made contact with his skull immediately before everything went black and he collapsed to the ground.

Jensen was on his feet again, and George Kim was slowly rising to his knees and shaking his head to gather his senses.

'But why? Who?' George Kim was gibbering with obvious fear as sirens blared in the distance.

'Let's just say Adrian sent me.'

George Kim was suddenly engulfed in fear. *Adrian!* Why hadn't he just disappeared as he'd planned to? What on earth had he been thinking?

Jensen also said this as he first restrained and then picked up the Chinese man with ease. After checking that Jackson was breathing and did not look to be badly injured, Jensen and Sanderson headed off at a trot to their hire car around the corner.

Chapter 124

Jason Jones was first to arrive on the scene followed closely by the heavily armed squad that Inspector Joel Franklin had at his disposal. He located Tom Jackson around the side of the house to the rear, lying on his back and holding his now-bleeding head. Others made their way into the house through the open rear door and searched the house room by room. They quickly established that whoever had been trying to break in had gone.

The officer across the road had been rendered unconscious and secured to his steering wheel by cable ties. He was coming to, and the trained paramedic in the squad established that he had not been permanently injured.

The paramedic was redirected to care for Tom as he suspected he may have concussion. They helped Jackson sit up, and he leaned on the back wall of the house while his head was bandaged.

Jackson spoke first. 'I heard two men struggling out the back. One said to the other, "George Kim, I presume". I ran out the back door, knocking the man who had spoken to the ground. After a brief tussle with both men, I had the situation under control before a third man, a big bastard, nearly bashed my head in with some sort of fighting stick. I thought I was done for. Oh, that's right, one more thing.' Tom's head still throbbed with pain but his thoughts were returning to him. 'I heard through the fog something like, "Let's just say Adrian sent me".'

'George Kim? Are you kidding me? And who the hell is Adrian? Adrian who?' The questions were flying from Jones.

'I don't know about Adrian, but I do know who George Kim is.' Jackson was livid that this thug had had the nerve to try and take him out in his own home.

Just then, Tom's iPhone pinged with the arrival of a new email. He glanced at his inbox absentmindedly as he was still thinking through the possibilities. His focus was immediately drawn to the subject heading on the email: George Kim.

Jackson put up his hand for all to cease talking while he quickly scanned the email. 'You're not going to believe this.'

Jones and the head of the police squad said, 'Believe what?' almost in unison.

'The email I just received is headed George Kim.' They all fell silent. 'It goes on to say, "Dear Mr Jackson, sorry to have interrupted your Saturday morning. I have been sent from far away to invite Mr Kim to a discussion with some of his colleagues. They are, shall we say, not at all pleased with his recent performances on behalf of the syndicate. They have authorised me to tell you that, even though not fatal to their operations, the closure of the casino in Hong Kong will be a major inconvenience. In their view, George Kim is solely responsible for their loss. They recognise, and respect, the role you have played in this, and want me to tell you that they bear you no ill will. You and yours are safe, and can go about your business, without the need for police protection. George Kim will not be able to bother you, or anyone else for that matter, again. The man across the road was rendered unconscious by relatively harmless means and he will recover quickly, if he hasn't already. You weren't meant to be involved and we hope you recover quickly from the bump on your head." There is no sign off, and the sender's email address is a weird mix of letters and numbers.'

Tom sat down. *Could this be true?* he wondered. He passed his iPhone to Jack, who passed it on to the squad leader. Each read the email and wondered if it could be that simple.

Chapter 125

Murray Jensen wasted no time in returning to the international airport. His chartered jet had been refuelled and was on standby, with a flight plan to Pnom Penh in Cambodia already filed. They would fly via Pnom Penh in an effort to throw the authorities off their scent. The flight plan from Pnom Penh to Hong Kong would not be as readily discoverable. It would allow Murray time to deliver his cargo to the location selected by Adrian, and return to London.

He had thought Adrian's idea of sending an untraceable email to Tom Jackson a brilliant one. It would immediately take the pressure off, even if its contents weren't believed. Tom would wish it to be so, and would make every effort to verify both source and content.

'Sit tight, George. It won't be long before you are home, safe and sound. Well, home anyway.' Murray laughed at his own joke and was joined by Charles.

*

George Kim was still in shock at what he had allowed to happen. First he had underestimated Tom Jackson, then Murray Jensen, and now his fellow syndicate members. *I have to figure a way through this. There's always a way.* Kim gritted his teeth in anger as he sat rigid in his comfortable chair in the private jet.

Chapter 126

Jones stayed with Tom for most of the rest of the day, just to make sure there were no adverse impacts from his concussion. Jones had been on the phone to Inspector Franklin several times.

After the third call he said, 'Sorry, Tom, but the coppers have no idea who they were and where the bastards may have gone. There have been plenty of flights in and out of Brisbane yesterday and today. These guys are bloody good, mate. The police haven't even been able to confirm George Kim's arrival, and there is no trace of the other people whatsoever. For now, we'll just have to accept what they've said in the email, but only time will tell of course.'

As Jones was leaving late in the afternoon, he noticed the double police presence across the road that Joel Franklin had reinstated, for now.

Chapter 127

One month later

Richard Black was found guilty at an expedited trial of participating in an international fraud to launder illegal monies and was jailed for ten years with no potential for early parole. The charges against him as an accomplice to murder were dropped by the police due to insufficient evidence.

Richard had desperately wanted to implicate both Murray Jensen and his fellow syndicate members, but was well aware that this would put his personal safety in jeopardy. He would not be safe in jail. He decided that he would prefer to remain alive so said nothing to implicate any of his colleagues.

He would have plenty of time to plan his revenge.

George Kim was heavily interrogated by his fellow syndicate members in Hong Kong. They wanted to learn from his mistakes, and so spent some time with him analysing what had transpired. Kim was then dispatched when it was determined that he had outlived his usefulness.

Miles Fletcher found a way to corrupt the findings of the forensic audit of Tom Jackson's work and private email accounts. With Roger Everingham out of the way, he was completely free to pursue his self-promotional activities at the firm in any manner he thought fit. He would no longer be weighed down by the burden of completely unpredictable and at times irrational baggage, which was an integral part of working with Everingham.

Murray Jensen collected a significant fee for returning George Kim to Hong Kong, then he ceased all action on the file. His instructions from Adrian were very clear. It was, after all, just business to Murray.

Sarina George enjoyed her role for Murray Jensen so much that, with Murray's encouragement, she returned to London to take up a full-time role in his European operations.

Tom Jackson was able to put together a legitimate syndicate of local and international banks to fund the Pacific Property Edward Street project. Documenting the transaction kept him and his team busy for many months. He remained a partner at Ridgeway Mason, fighting an often-daily battle with some of his partners. Tom enjoyed the practise of law, and he particularly enjoyed nurturing and teaching members of his team. More importantly, he had resumed regular contact with Mary. Both were optimistic about the prospect of a reconciliation between them and hopeful of a less chaotic period ahead.

Little did Jackson know this was going to be very short lived indeed.

Acknowledgements

Many thanks to my editor and independent publisher Dr Juliette Lachemeier from the Erudite Pen, for your structural ideas and other editorial input, which were both timely and invaluable. Your passion and dedication to detail is extraordinary. Thank you for all your support and encouragement.

It would be remiss of me to not also thank our good friend Julie Comans for the introduction to Juliette.

Thank you to Judith San Nicolas for the amazing book cover.

Thanks also to all who've read my first novel. I hope you enjoyed reading the book as much as I enjoyed writing it.

ABOUT THE AUTHOR

Hailing from Australia, Rod Besley's unique background as an esteemed lawyer infuses his writing with a deep understanding of legal intricacies. His ability to unravel complex legal puzzles while keeping readers on the edge of their seats is a testament to his expertise and narrative finesse.

As the creative force behind *Know Your Enemy*, Rod invites readers to explore the high-stakes world of corporate transactions, espionage and unrelenting suspense. He has a knack for weaving intricate plots and delivering heart-pounding twists for legal-thriller enthusiasts. In the style of James Patterson, his novels deliver short, sharp chapters that are jam packed with action, intrigue and suspense.

Follow Rod's literary journey for a glimpse into the mind of a legal virtuoso turned storyteller. With each new release, he invites readers to dive headfirst into the realms of power, corruption and the relentless pursuit of truth. If you're a fan of gripping legal dramas that defy conventions, Rod's novels are a must-read for your bookshelf.

The author graduated with a combined law/accounting degree from the Australian National University. He has over thirty-five years of experience at prestigious law firms as a transaction lawyer. As a partner, he was regularly exposed to the 'cut and thrust' of huge transactions in one of the largest global law firms.

A skilled legal wordsmith and keen assessor of human behaviour, Rod now utilises this talent in fiction writing – developing characters and plots for legal thrillers.

Know Your Enemy: A Tom Jackson Legal Thriller is Rod's first novel in the Tom Jackson series. Jackson is an esteemed transaction lawyer who becomes embroiled in an illegally funded multi-billion-dollar development project. Know Your Enemy, although entirely fictional, gives readers an insight into the high-stakes world of corporate transactions, espionage, intimidation and conspiracy.

Enjoyed the book? You can contact the author at:

Email: rod.besley88@gmail.com

Facebook: Rod Besley Author:
https://www.facebook.com/profile.php?id=61550080172957

If you liked the book, please leave a review on Amazon, Goodreads or with the author directly. Reviews are invaluable in supporting an author's hard work and are greatly appreciated.

www.ingramcontent.com/pod-product-compliance
Lightning Source LLC
Chambersburg PA
CBHW020005140726
47904CB00018B/1884